Falling
Boy

Also by Alison McGhee

Rainlight

Shadow Baby

Was It Beautiful?

All Rivers Flow to the Sea

Someday (and Peter H. Reynolds)

Falling Boy

Alison McGhee

Picador · New York

www.picadorusa.com

Picador® is a U.S. registered trademark and is used by St. Martin's Press under license from Pan Books Limited.

For information on Picador Reading Group Guides, as well as ordering, please contact Picador.
Phone: 646-307-5629
Fax: 212-253-9627
E-mail: readinggroupguides@picadorusa.com

Grateful acknowledgment is made for permission to reprint excerpts from the following:

"Musée des Beaux Arts," copyright © 1940 and renewed 1968 by W. H. Auden, from *Collected Poems* by W. H. Auden. Used by permission of Random House, Inc.

"Failing and Flying," from *Refusing Heaven* by Jack Gilbert, published in 2005 by Alfred A. Knopf, a division of Random House, Inc.

Library of Congress Cataloging-in-Publication Data

McGhee, Alison, 1960–
    Falling boy : a novel / by Alison McGhee.—1st Picador ed.
        p. cm.
    ISBN-13: 978-0-312-42592-0
    ISBN-10: 0-312-42592-9
    1. Accident victims—Fiction.   2. Teenagers with disabilities—Fiction.   3. Teenagers—Fiction.   4. Coming of age—Fiction.   5. Minneapolis (Minn.)—Fiction.   I. Title.

PS3563.C36378F36 2007
813'.54—dc22

                                                                    2006036762

First Edition: March 2007

10   9   8   7   6   5   4   3   2   1

To Luke O'Brien,
whose unexpected answer to
my superhero question
gave me the pivotal perspective
from which I wrote the book

In Brueghel's Icarus, for instance: how everything turns away
Quite leisurely from the disaster; the ploughman may
Have heard a splash, the forsaken cry,
But for him it was not an important failure; the sun shone
As it had to on the white legs disappearing into the green
Water; and the expensive delicate ship that must have seen
Something amazing, a boy falling out of the sky,
Had somewhere to get to and sailed calmly on.

—from "Musée des Beaux Arts" by W. H. Auden

...Icarus was not failing as he fell,
But just coming to the end of his triumph.

—from "Failing and Flying" by Jack Gilbert

Falling
Boy

One

They spent their lives in search of sweetness, these bees: blue morning glories climbing the trellis outside the bakery window, a half-empty packet of sugar, the shallow bowls of lemonade that Joseph set on each table.

Joseph dipped his finger in a bowl and held it out, a perch in a birdcage. The bee drifted through the bakery on the summer air, drifted past the table of toddlers and their mothers, drifted past the skinny child Enzo in her brown velvet chair in the corner, drifted past Zap, who was bent over the cash register behind the counter. Joseph willed the bee toward himself: Come, hungry bee, here is sugar for you.

It was the end of June and the air of Minneapolis lay heavy and slow on Joseph's skin. Even if he rose at dawn to push his way around the lake, the breeze was languid, saturated.

Joseph held his syrupy finger straight and still. He stilled his breathing and waited for the bee, which seemed to have neither buzz nor any visible means of keeping itself aloft, that heavy body, threadlike legs hanging limp and useless.

"Is that the hero guy?" the little boy in the Batman shirt said, and pointed at Joseph. "Is that him?"

His Batman shirt was frayed at the bottom where he rolled it with his thumb and forefinger. Dark dribbles on the chest. His friend, the one who always wore a yellow windbreaker, stared at Joseph.

"You don't always have to say everything twice," Batman's mother said. "And boys, don't stare at people. It's rude. Be quiet and eat your blueberry muffins."

She glanced at Joseph herself and at once glanced away. She and the mother of the windbreaker boy nodded at each other. Joseph held his finger so still as to appear stone; the bee alighted on Joseph's finger and huddled itself, focused and greedy, onto Joseph's first knuckle.

"But is he the hero that the beer guy was talking about? Is he?"

"You can tell for yourself, can't you, Batman?" Zap said. "Look at him."

Batman and his friend, Windbreaker Boy, gazed silently in the direction of Joseph. Zap kept working, extracting crumpled bills from the cash register and smoothing them into piles. Joseph's finger held steady. Another bee circled, and another.

"Watch him closely now," Zap said. "Note his every action."

Batman's mother frowned at Zap. What was he doing, encouraging these children to stare at people when she had just told them it was rude? Zap looked at her and held his finger to his lips: Shhh. All is well. Let me do my job.

"What's he doing, Zap? What's he doing?"

"See for yourself, Batman," Zap said. "Observe the boy. And observe the bee."

The word *bee*, and Enzo, who loathed bees, looked up from her table and hunched back in her chair, her mechanical pencil held in front of her like a shield. Zap took a black felt marker from the pen mug and wrote WE ARE IN SORE NEED OF FIVES on a napkin. He taped the napkin to the penny cup and faced it outward.

The lone bee on Joseph's finger lifted itself into the air and zagged away toward the open doors.

"See?" Zap said. "The boy finds himself surrounded by bees. But do the bees sting the boy?"

Joseph wiped his finger on his jeans. The bee bowl at this table was filled to the brim; lemonade overflowed when Joseph opened the napkin dispenser to refill it.

"They do not," Zap said. "The boy remains unstung."

Refilling napkin dispensers was tricky. Fill one too full and the napkins were impossible to remove. Without the click of the latch after refilling, the napkins would fall out. Now Joseph took a damp sponge in one hand, lifted the small bowl of lemonade with the other, and wiped clean the puddle. Bees hovered over the sweet vanished spill.

"Does that mean he's a superhero, Zap?" Batman said. "Does it?"

"Indeed it does, Batman," Zap said. "A superhero is in our midst, and his name is Joseph. Joseph the beekeeper."

Batman nodded. He stuck his index and middle fingers in his mouth. Windbreaker Boy shook his head.

"No," Windbreaker Boy announced. "That guy can't be a superhero. He's in a wheelchair."

The two mothers turned as one, fingers already to lips.

"Boys, shhh. Never talk about people in front of them like that."

"But he's in a wheelchair."

Joseph rolled to the next table, where someone had emptied the napkin dispenser of its entire stack. This someone had used the stack of napkins as a makeshift notebook and had covered the napkins with penciled numbers. What did the numbers mean? Was someone out there just now realizing that he had left his numbered napkins at the bakery and was this someone filled with anger and frustration?

"Wheelchair, wheelchair, wheelchair," Windbreaker Boy chanted. He gazed at the mothers, brimming with the power of the forbidden word, and the mothers glared and hissed.

Batman looked from his friend to Zap and back again. He took his fingers out of his mouth.

"The beer guy said the beekeeper guy was a hero. But I don't like the beer guy."

"The beer guy is the beekeeper's father," Zap said. "And you don't have to like him for him to be right. This one time anyway."

"A hero can't be in a wheelchair," Windbreaker Boy insisted.

"Oh, but that is where you are sadly mistaken, my small windbreaker friend."

Batman and Windbreaker Boy stared at Joseph in his wheelchair, and Enzo too stared at Joseph from her table in the corner. Her mechanical pencil, which she called a click-ster, bounced up and down, secured between her second and third fingers. As long as other children were nearby, Enzo would not venture forth. She would remain in her corner and bide her time.

"How can the bee guy be a hero?" Windbreaker Boy said. "Heroes fly. Heroes wear capes. Heroes wear tights."

Zap ripped open a bag of ice cubes. The bakery's ice maker was broken, and until it was fixed they were buying bags of ice from Rainbow Foods and keeping them in the freezer. Each summer day required several bags of ice, under the lemonade and orange juice, in the watercooler, nested around the cream and milk carafes.

"The beekeeper is a hero because he risked life and limb to rescue his mother from a fate worse than death," Zap said. "She was stranded on a precipice, and with no thought to his own safety, the beekeeper crept out onto thin air."

"He must have had a cape, then," Windbreaker Boy said.

"What's a precipice?" Batman said.

"A precipice is a cliff."

Batman and Windbreaker Boy studied Joseph with this new knowledge. Enzo watched and absorbed from her table, clickster motionless between thumb and index finger.

"A cliff on a mountain overlooking the sea," Zap elabo-rated. It was his habit to tell superhero stories to the children in the bakery. "The sea surrounding their island."

"Is the beekeeper from an island?"

Zap nodded. "All hail the beekeeper," he said. "All hail Joseph, the beekeeper from the island of bees."

Batman and Windbreaker Boy studied Joseph. Now they

were kneeling on the seats of their wooden chairs. The mothers had relaxed and turned away into their own soft conversation. They were free to release their reign; Zap had led their children into questions and contemplation. Blueberry muffins sat half-eaten on the table.

Overhead, the big bakery fans whirred, slicing the air with long wooden blades. Their thin dangling chains clanked faintly in the manufactured breeze. Joseph could reach the wall switch that controlled the fans, but the chains hung far above his head. Even tall Zap had a hard time reaching them.

"Keep watching, my small friends," Zap said. "And perhaps, if you are lucky, you too will someday unlock the secret of the bees."

"But why's he in that wheelchair?" Windbreaker Boy said. He was a boy who would not be dissuaded. His gaze was truculent and unconvinced. "What's wrong with him?"

The mothers turned back, both swarming on Batman and Windbreaker Boy. Don't point. Keep your voice down. We don't ask questions like that. We don't stare at handicapped people. That's rude. Rude! Finish your muffin now; it's time to go.

"The Mighty Thor has been watching and listening," Enzo said to Joseph, "and now she knows three things about you."

Batman and Windbreaker Boy were gone in a shuffle of trash gathering and feet dragging and shoe tying. The bakery was empty except for Enzo and Joseph and Zap, who was stacking paper cups and their lids by the coffee carafes: small, medium, large. Enzo pointed her clickster at Joseph's head.

"Number one, you have very long hair for a boy."

Joseph saw Zap turn his head in their direction. Zap was bat-eared. The sound of Enzo's voice echoed off him and he could locate its precise origin no matter where she was in the large bakery room, no matter when she had slipped in, no matter how many other customers were there.

"So do I," Zap said. "What's your point?"

Enzo ignored him and lowered her voice.

"Number two, the bee thing."

She nodded significantly, as if she had divined a secret unknown to anyone else.

"Number three, you refuse to talk about your past. These are the things that the Mighty Thor has noticed."

She leveled the clickster at Joseph's heart. *Click*.

"Stop calling yourself the Mighty Thor," Zap said. "I'm sick of it."

"Shut up," Enzo said. "This is a private conversation between the beekeeper and me."

She refused to speak directly to Zap, her sworn enemy. Enzo wiggled her clickster. She was only nine but she knew how to level a stern gaze, and she did so often. An untouched raisin scone sat on Enzo's table. Joseph had taken the raisin scone from its basket in the muffin-and-scone bakery case earlier and placed it before her on a doily, but she had ignored its presence.

Enzo pointed her clickster at Joseph's forehead.

"Did you really rescue your mother from a fate worse than death on a cliff overlooking the sea?"

"No."

"Did you really creep out onto thin air?"

"No."

"Did you really fly?"

"No."

"Answer me," Enzo said.

"I am answering you."

"No, *really* answer me."

Joseph saw that she would not be happy until the answer to her questions was yes. Yes was the answer she sought. *Yes*, Joseph had crept out onto thin air and *yes* he had flown and *yes* he had rescued his mother from a fate worse than death. She was a child who longed for yes.

Enzo pointed the clickster at Joseph's heart. *Click.*

Zap had folded his arms across his chest and was watching Enzo, the bee child buzzing around the silent Joseph. Zap was only seventeen, one year older than Joseph, but he was capable of appearing older. Joseph reached for the saltshaker on Enzo's table and unscrewed the lid. He poured in a thin stream of white from the large canister in his lap. His movements were slow and deliberate, the better to calm the angry child. Enzo darted a glance at the raisin scone, plump and still on its doily.

Joseph rolled to the next table and unscrewed the top of its small glass saltshaker. Enzo followed.

"Answer me," Enzo chanted. "Answer me."

"No," Joseph said again. "No, no, and no."

Enzo squinched up her face and put her hands over her ears and sang "Lalalalalala." From the counter where he now stood sifting through the bowl of Auntie Apple's caramels, Zap frowned at her. A bee drifted over and hovered above Enzo, seeming not even to move as it hung in the air above her chanting head. Enzo and Zap were like bees themselves, angry and bumbling in each other's presence, enemies forced to coexist in a single hive. Enzo brandished her clickster, slashing it back and forth in the air. She took aim at Zap.

"*Pow*," she muttered.

It took very little to set Enzo off. When she was angry, she muttered or spoke in a controlled yell. Zap narrowed his eyes at Enzo, who ignored him the way no other child did. Zap was a Pied Piper, tall and strong. Small children looked at him as a magical adult, an adult who was on their side. They called him Zap because he told them stories about superheroes. Zap saved broken cookies for them in tiny paper cups, which he passed out on the sly.

But Enzo?

Enzo too was a child, but Enzo alone ignored the sound of Zap's flute. Enzo alone was left outside the mountain after the door had closed, the other children inside with the magic Zap, and when he was with Enzo, Zap too was without laughter, without music.

Zap turned away and began bagging unsold day-old bread for the food-shelf man, who arrived daily at four o'clock. It was the food-shelf man's habit to stride without stopping to the day-old shelf for the bagged loaves. If the food-shelf man didn't see them waiting, he turned and strode out again. It was a point of pride with Zap always to be prepared for the food-shelf man.

"Bee," Enzo whispered. She pointed at a hovering wasp and followed its wavering progress with her clickster.

The child lived in fear of bees, and she did not distinguish among them. Wasps, hornets, honeybees, bumblebees, all were the same to her, and in her presence, Joseph had also come to regard all bees as one bee. But bees were everywhere, hoisting themselves into the air from underground, swarming around their papery hives. This one drank its fill and then dragged itself back into the air, drifting first toward the coffee station with its two urns—French roast and decaf French roast—and then suddenly darting toward the open door.

Enzo unshrank herself and returned to her familiar shape, nine-year-old girl sitting straight up on a lumpy velvet chair. She clicked her clickster.

"Stop clicking that thing," Zap said. "It's driving me crazy."

"My clickster is essential to this investigation," Enzo said in the voice of a calm professional trained to deal with recalcitrant witnesses.

An enormously tall man wearing a kilt stood outside the far window, looking in at Enzo in her brown velvet chair. He often came to the bakery in the late afternoon, seeking Zap, who gave him hard-boiled eggs. Hard-boiled eggs were the only thing that the man in the kilt would eat.

Enzo made shooing motions at him.

"Go away," she said. "No eggs for you today."

"Leave Kilt Man alone," Zap said.

Kilt Man gazed at Enzo as if he sensed her presence but could not quite see her. Enzo pushed her hands at the air as if she could propel the tall man away by force of air and will.

"Hey, Kilt Man," she cried. "Kilt Man, fly away home. Your house is on fire and your children are alone."

"Cut it out," Zap said. "The poor guy's a loony tune."

"Shut up."

Zap moved from behind the counter to Enzo's table and bent over, knelt so that he was on her level. She turned her head away. The man in the kilt stood still and straight, his pallid face calm.

"I'm asking you please to leave him alone," Zap said. "Please, Enzo."

"Mighty Thor."

Enzo kept her head turned and rigid. Zap sighed and backed away, toward the counter where the day-old bread was waiting. The man in the kilt angled his own head down, a slow and stunted movement. Now he was looking directly at Enzo. Now he could both sense her and see her. His world had opened a crack and allowed her presence entry.

"He should take medicine," Enzo said.

"If he took medicine," Joseph said, "he might feel like he was disappearing."

"He *should* disappear."

Enzo was clenched, anger shimmering out. It happened so easily. It took nothing to set her off; the sight of Kilt Man outside the window, gazing into her world from his, was enough. She hunched forward in her Kilt Man stance, neck held rigid and eyes unblinking and lips moving. Zap stood behind the counter, breaking giant day-old cookies into small pieces, his small-child stack of Dixie cups teetering beside him.

"Maybe he likes being crazy," Zap said to Enzo. "Ever think of that?"

"How could anyone like being crazy?"

Zap was looking at Joseph; Joseph could feel it—but he did not look back at Zap. Did anyone like being crazy? Did anyone choose?

"Make him go away. He's scary. I'm scared of him."

Enzo's voice was high and thin, a whine, a plea. Make him go away. Make the man in the kilt leave the window, the sidewalk outside, the bakery, world of sweetness, where bread and pastry and cakes rose high and light in the burning heat of the dawn ovens, ovens hidden away in the back room. Disappear the man in the kilt, so that no small child would have to see him.

Joseph's hands clenched on the tires of his chair. If he shoved backward, he would crash, crash into the table behind him, the table where a father and his son sat, the father reading the paper, the son squeaking his straw in and out of the hole in the cover of his plastic cup. Squeak. Squeak. Now the father looked up from his paper. The son kept squeaking, but the father folded his paper with a snap and frowned at the man outside the window, the man in the kilt who craved eggs. No eggs for you today, Kilt Man. Take your brain with its flying misfirings and go away. You make no sense. Leave us alone.

Joseph inched backward in his chair. He stared at the father, who was staring out the window, and willed him to look away from Kilt Man. The father drummed his fingers on the table and frowned. Joseph rolled silently backward another inch. The boy squeaked his straw up and down in a swift and complicated rhythm.

Kilt Man looked through the window at Joseph, silent in his inching chair. Enzo sat next to him in her own chair, index fingers held up and together in the sign that was supposed to ward off evil. She was saying something, but Joseph couldn't hear her. His gaze held the gaze of the man in the kilt. Now the father was saying something to his son. Stop that squeaking; it's time to go. Now the boy was protesting. *Make him go away.* Beyond the bakery was the world outside, where the kilted man with the sad eyes stood. Anger and fear buzzed within the world of the bakery, ricocheting from wall to wall.

There was no escape. You could not leave one world without being trapped in the next. Joseph's neck was hurting; he had rolled himself against the straw-squeaking boy's table and his hands were still pushing at the tires, shoving the chair against the hard wooden table edge.

Breathe.

John Schaefer from rehab used to say that. "Breathe, my child," he would say when he saw Joseph tensing. "Breathe."

Joseph lifted his hands from the tires and set them in his lap, fingers twined around one another like the slender twining trunks of birch trees.

Breathe, my child.

The father and son disappeared down the sidewalk, the boy still protesting, his bent straw clutched in one hand.

Breathe.

Zap stared at Joseph from behind the counter, worry in his eyes, while his hands kept busy with their broken-cookie task. In Joseph's peripheral vision, the tall shadow of Kilt Man moved backward down the sidewalk and faded away.

"I'm scared of him," Enzo said again.

"The beekeeper isn't scared of him, though," Zap said. "That's what makes him the hero."

"I told you I wasn't a hero," Joseph said.

His own voice sounded strange to Joseph, rusty from disuse. He needed to clear his throat. He needed to clear his brain.

Enzo briskly clicked her clickster and made her eyes large and unblinking.

"Back to my investigation," she said. "Did the beer guy chase your mother to the edge of the cliff, and is that why you had to rescue your mother? Is that what really happened?"

"No."

"Well, what was she doing on the cliff, then? Was she trying to escape the bees?"

Joseph said nothing.

"Was . . . she . . . trying . . . to escape . . . the bees?" Enzo said in the overly enunciated tones of an angry parent.

"Maybe she was trying to escape a bratty kid who wouldn't stop asking her questions," Zap said. "Ever think of that?"

Enzo ignored him. "Do you have a brother?"

"No," Joseph said.

"A sister?"

"No."

"No, really," Enzo said. "Do you have a sister?"

She was doing it again, lost in her world of yes longing.

"No," Zap said. "You heard him the first time."

Enzo pointed the clickster at Joseph and clicked once, as if he were withholding information that she would wrest from him sooner or later.

"So it's just you, then," she said. "You and the beer guy and your mother."

"No," Zap said. "It's just him and Big. No mother."

"Yes mother," Joseph said.

Zap stared from the bread rack.

"Yes mother," Joseph said again.

Enzo's clickster did a small victory dance in the air. Her questions had provoked a reaction, a confrontation, however small; the investigator was on the right track. Joseph looked away from her eyes, which were bright with triumph.

"But she's not here," Zap said. He was looking right at Joseph, but Joseph would not look at him.

"She's in the hospital," Joseph said.

"Right," Zap said. "That's all I meant. I didn't mean that you don't have a mother. I only meant that your mother isn't here, in this particular upper-midwestern part of the world."

"Your mother is in the hospital?" Enzo said. "Tell us about her."

Joseph watched his fingers twine on themselves again. Now his fingers were playing a game his mother used to play with him when he was little. He looked at the dull mass of fingers and chose one. *Lift*, he commanded the finger; *raise yourself into the air*. He watched as the wrong finger detached itself from the mass and rose. *No. Not you.* He refocused on the finger he wanted. *Lift.* Again the wrong finger rose. Synapses were firing, but they were misfiring. Commands were not reaching the desired target.

"Come on," Enzo wheedled. "Talk."

No. Joseph would not talk. He would hold in everything swarming inside him about his mother. No one in this new world would know anything about her, how every day they played Scrabble together, how she wore three tiny earrings in the shape of lipsticks on one ear and three tiny earrings in the shape of mouths on the other, how her dark winter coat had been a gift from Big one Christmas and she loved it because the sleeves were long enough and the fake fur around the collar and cuffs kept her warm, how the coat had come with two large brown buttons in a tiny plastic bag hidden in the pocket and his mother had held up the buttons and said, "Two, not one, that's class."

Now Joseph's shoulders were curved around his chest. He would clench himself tight. He would hold his mother within and he would not think about her, alone now in the hospital, near no one who had seen her fingering the two extra buttons of her dark coat, no one who knew her, no one who held her heart within his own.

Enzo retrained the clickster on Joseph and made her bright eyes flat and hard, as if she were a detective schooled to give away nothing.

"New subject. How did your legs get hurt?"

"His legs don't hurt," Zap said.

"He's in a wheelchair. Of course they do."

"Of course they don't. It's called paralysis. Ever heard of it?"

The door behind the counter opened and a short, wide man appeared in the doorway and beckoned to Zap. Zap rolled his eyes and pushed himself away from the table. Frank the Figurehead occasionally emerged from the back to confer with his son. In the three weeks he had been working there, it seemed to Joseph that Zap ran the bakery, but the Figurehead was Zap's father and the owner, and when he beckoned, Zap answered the call.

Enzo turned her back on him and pointed her clickster at Joseph's legs. Now she had the subject all to herself.

"I repeat my question. How did your legs get hurt?"

"My legs don't hurt."

Joseph prodded himself in the thighs with both index fingers and invited her with a gesture to do the same. Enzo shook her head. No. She would not touch Joseph's legs. That was not the job of the investigator. Joseph rolled to the last table, where the last saltshaker needed filling.

"How long will your mother be in the hospital?" Enzo said suddenly.

Her eyes bored into Joseph's. She moved her head back and forth in a metronomic sway, as if she were trying to hypnotize him. She stood up and moved behind Joseph's wheelchair and placed her hands on the back grips.

"A long time."

Enzo gave his chair a little push.

"You must not be a very good superhero if your mother's in the hospital."

"I already told you that I'm not a hero at all. That's Zap's story, not mine."

She pushed his chair again.

"A real superhero would fix his legs," she said. "Then he'd go rescue his mother. That's what a real superhero would do."

Joseph watched his fingers, holding the saltshaker at a slant. The white salt streamed into the opened top. If he listened carefully enough, he might hear the sound it made, tiny cubes of white tumbling one over the other into the darkness of the interior of the saltshaker. Hush. Listen. Anything in this world might be making a sound at any given moment, and anyone listening might find import in that sound. If you only listened, meaning that had been lost might be found. That was what Joseph had always believed. But he was in an unfamiliar world now, and he no longer knew if those words were words he could still live by.

Again Enzo nudged his chair. She smelled like her hair, child's hair of shampoo and sun, and of cinnamon.

"Don't you miss her?"

Push.

Enzo leaned in close, and closer. Her T-shirt was damp with sweat.

"Don't you?"

Push.

The saltshaker fell to the floor with a flat splat: broken. White grains spilled out, whiter than the white tiles. Joseph felt his legs gathering themselves to tense, to spring, to rise from the chair and fling him out the double doors, down the block, west to Lake Calhoun, to run down the stairs to the lake three at a time. He would leap over the bikers and Rollerbladers, jump to the lowest branch of the huge old oak by the 32nd Street playground, and turn himself east, away from the plains, back to the hushed old mountains from whence he had come. He would aim the arrow of his body at the redbrick buildings of Utica, at the redbrick building of the hospital. The doors of the hospital would open as he approached and he would wing his way to his mother's room, and alight beside her bed, or by her chair, or find her in the hallway, crouched behind a ficus tree, those trees condemned to live indoors in office buildings and hospitals.

I am here now were the words he would beam silently to her, and she would hear him, and her hand would emerge from the old dark coat with two, not one, extra buttons that long ago had been wrapped in red-and-green Santa Claus paper and reach toward him.

"Because I would," Enzo said. "I would miss my mother every day of my life."

Joseph hunched forward in his chair. The little bowl of lemonade on the table before him crawled and shuddered with bees, their wings lifting and settling.

Two

"What the hell happened here?" Zap said to Enzo. "What did you do, idiot child?"

Zap was back and the Figurehead was gone. The clickster was balanced between Enzo's index and middle fingers.

"I was just asking him about his mother," Enzo said.

"Well, don't."

"It's a free country," Enzo said. "I can ask him about anything I want. Anyway, you're the one who started it. You're the one who said he was trying to save his mother."

Joseph stared at his feet trapped in their white cotton socks, tied into the running shoes that he had brought with him from the land of mountains, where he no longer lived. He was still in his chair. He had not flown.

"You made him disappear again," Zap said. "Idiot child."

"My name is not Idiot Child. My name is the Mighty Thor. And guess what? You were wrong. His legs do so hurt. He was pounding them. So there."

Joseph heard in her voice that she was close to tears. It was early evening in the bakery and the long rays of the summer sun slanted across the bakery cases.

"You can't be the Mighty Thor," Zap said.

"Yes I can."

"No you can't. The Mighty Thor was a comic book superhero from the seventies."

Enzo's hand clenched around her clickster.

"You could be the Unmighty Thor, though," Zap said. "That would be a good name for you."

Back and forth their words darted, spears of anger and frustration flung from one to the other. The enemy bees spoke to each other by means of harsh buzzes. They spoke with furiously beating wings. If Enzo could, she would zoom up into the air and scrape herself along the pressed-tin ceiling of the bakery. She would hurt herself and be glad of the hurt.

Joseph sat in his chair and looked at his hands. Once they gripped the tires this tightly, it was hard to let them go. Hard to ungrip. He willed the index fingers first to relax, to soften, to feel the rubber of the tire. Then the thumbs. Then the rest of them. Let go, Joseph soothed, let go. One by one, his fingers loosened.

Now Joseph's hands hung by the sides of the tires. Now he could turn to the child. He was the beekeeper and he could work his calming beekeeper magic.

"Enzo," Joseph said.

Zap and Enzo both turned to Joseph. The child's eyes

were too bright. They threatened to overflow, but Enzo held the tears back, and Joseph could feel in his own eyes how mighty was her effort. The raisin scone he had brought her still sat on her table.

"Welcome back from the island, beekeeper," Zap said.

"Enzo," Joseph said again.

Zap gave up. He turned and went back to the counter and opened up the cash register.

"Not Enzo," Enzo said. "Mighty Thor."

Her voice was dull. Not-Enzo gazed at Joseph from a land she had willed into being, a land where the name Mighty Thor belonged to her alone and not a seventies comic book superhero. Joseph knew by the way she whispered it that Enzo loved the name she had chosen. She wanted to be known not as Enzo, idiot child, but as Thor, child of might. Joseph sat in his chair and kept his eyes on hers. Come back, Mighty Thor. Come back to the bakery, where a raisin scone waits for you at your table in the corner, your table and your brown velvet chair.

"I am not a superhero," Joseph said.

She shook her head, her eyes filling. She wanted to hear yes, but Joseph was telling her no. He had to keep telling her no.

"But why not? Why can't you be?"

"I failed in my mission, that's why."

"But the beer guy said. He *said.*"

The child was staring at him with her too-bright eyes. The child was hungry. The child was tired. The child was standing on a cliff, trying to keep her balance.

"Mighty Thor," Joseph said.

He sent the magic words—Mighty Thor—out to Enzo,

the child who was trying not to cry. Zap, behind the counter, was silent, his eyes moving between Enzo and Joseph.

"Mighty Thor," Joseph said again. "What if you yourself were a superhero? Imagine that."

The child gazed back at him.

"What would your superpower be, do you think?"

The tight lines of her shoulders began to droop. She kept her eyes on him and shook her head. This was the way to call her home. Joseph held his hand out to her and beckoned— Come, little child, come and tell me your secret—but no. Enzo would not budge. She, too, would say no.

"I could tell you," she said in the thin voice of someone who had memorized a line from a movie, "but then I'd have to kill you."

"We're closing," Zap called from the counter. "Calling all brats. Time to fly away to your brat caves."

Where did Enzo go when the bakery closed? She was there every day, moving in and out of the open double doors at will, flitting from table to bakery case to sidewalk, never alighting for long. The clickster was limp in her hand.

"Closing time," Zap called again. "Now."

He banged shut the cash register drawer. Time to let the register rest, and the muffins and cookies on their display doilies and plates, and the loaves of bread in their baskets. Time to let darkness soften the edges of the tables and smooth the worn treads of the black-and-white tiles of the floor. Time for the bees to return from their wanderings and huddle to-gether in darkness. Time for Joseph to glide to Enzo's table in the corner and pluck the raisin scone from its plate, glide back to where the child stood still fighting tears, and hold it out to her, that she might take it from his hand and carry it with her as she went out from the bakery and away, into the still summer night.

Joseph punched the handicap button with the stick he kept tucked next to him for that purpose, and the double doors of the gym opened with their squeak and groan. The *m* dangled off the end of the word *gym*. JIM'S GY . . . M. The *m* had been dangling ever since Joseph had left his home and moved to Minneapolis. Maybe the *m* had been dangling ever since the gym was built.

Joseph wheeled down the hall, past the man who didn't bother checking his membership card, the man who each night yawned and waved simultaneously.

Yawn.

Wave.

Joseph's black backpack swung and slapped gently at the back of his chair. He was already wearing his swimsuit. He left the house in it every day.

Joseph could swim at the Y on Hennepin Avenue, bright and windowed, but he didn't. The old guys at Jim's Gy . . . m lifted weights in a windowless room. No piped-in music, no televisions mounted overhead. The old guys grunted. The old guys had gray hair or no hair and heavy, wrinkled faces.

The pool was a squat rectangle filled with chalky blue water. No windows here, either. The weight room smelled of sweat and the pool room of chlorine, and old concrete, and damp wood from the single set of bleachers on the other side of the pool, the old-guy, non-Joseph side.

He rolled into the single handicapped stall, the stall with the crookedly hung door. Shoved his black backpack with his deodorant and extra T-shirt and catheter into the bottom of the locker. In his chair, he was not high enough to reach the single hook. He wrapped his towel around his shoulders. All of Big's towels were thin and dingy. At home in Utica, Joseph and his mother's towels had been blue and green, and he had washed them and folded them in thirds and kept them in the second drawer on the left in the bathroom.

Down the tiled hallway, into the windowless room of fake blue and acrid chlorine. An old guy was there. He sat on the edge of the pool, fumbling with a yellow bathing cap, the kind that old ladies wore, plain yellow and flowerless, even though he had no hair that Joseph could see. The old guy bent forward, dipped his hands into the water, and splashed tiny handfuls onto the skinny white legs. He tilted his head up at Joseph across the pool and appraised him.

"Kid! What the hell happened to you?"

Joseph put his towel on the bench. He rolled to the very edge of the pool, put on the brake, and lowered himself out and down. Not easy. Pay attention. Do not fall. "Falling isn't so bad once you've done it," John Schaefer had said back in Utica. "Make yourself fall," John Schaefer had said. "It's not the end of the world."

But Joseph did not want to fall.

"Kid! You deaf? What the hell happened to you?"

The water rippled up and over the filter.

"Not Vietnam. Too young. Right?"

Splash.

"Too young to have heard of Vietnam, probably. Ever hear of it? Vietnam."

Splash.

"Born that way? A cripple?"

Splash.

"No. I'm guessing not. Jesus Christ, then, I'm stumped. Stumped! Get it? No, wait. You still got legs, so you can't be stumped. Your legs just don't work. Am I right?"

Joseph lowered himself into the water.

"Oh Christ, kid, I got it. Muscular dystrophy. That's it, isn't it?"

Joseph twisted onto his back and stared up at the ceiling. Up and up and up, to where the fluorescent tubes of light hung blurry and white. Arms out. And in. And out. And in. He swam three laps and rested, his arms draped over the edge of the pool.

"Kid! Can you pee on your own, or do you use a bag?"

Joseph closed his eyes. He came to the pool for the blue silence of it, the cold wash of water at night. The pool was an island surrounded on all sides by the summer sounds of this city, this city of lakes, of Mississippi River, of summer storms that whirled themselves upward into sudden tornadoes. Here was the place where Joseph ended his days, the place from which he emerged wet and aching into the dark night air.

Big was sleeping now, in his small bedroom with the window shade duct-taped to the sill. He did not know that his son was swimming, pulling one arm over the other. Big would rise in a few hours, rise in the darkness and make his way to the darkened bakery, where he would enter the propped-open alley door and light the ovens.

The drive from Utica to Minneapolis had taken three days. It was late May and Joseph had been in rehab since February. John Schaefer had sat in the wide doorway of the lobby, nodding and drumming his fingers on his tires. The chair that Big had brought with him was folded up behind them in the cab of Big's pickup. Big drove with two hands on the wheel, as if he had studied a driver's manual diagram and noted the exact placement of each hand. Big didn't used to drive that way. He had been a hang one hand out the window type, a drive with your knees type if he needed to pull on a pair of gloves or light a cigarette, a habit he seemed to have given up in the year since he had left Joseph and his mother.

"You have to go?" his father had said into the silence, an hour into the drive.

John Schaefer must have told Big at the hospital that it was important to pay attention to toileting. He's in good shape for a para, John Schaefer might have told him. He's one of the lucky ones because he can take care of it himself, but you've got to stay on top of the toileting. Infection. UTIs are nasty things if you don't get on them right away.

"No."

"You sure?"

"I'm sure."

Now Joseph pushed off with his arms and began to swim again.

Arms out. And in.

"Kid!"

The old guy's voice was magnified and blurred by the water sloshing in and out of Joseph's ears. He stopped swimming and draped his arms over the pool's edge. The old guy stood on the other side, his yellow bathing cap askew. He tilted his head and surveyed Joseph.

"Got a girlfriend?"

Joseph shook his head.

"Why the hell not? You've got the looks."

The old guy hobbled along the edge of the pool, legs bracing on each step so as not to slip on the wet concrete.

"Got one for me, then? The wife passed on and I don't like being alone."

The old guy shuffled his way to the locker room door and waved. Back to the bat cave. Joseph pushed off with his arms and began again to do the backstroke. Arms out. Arms in.

"I'm John Schaefer, nice to meet you. You can still have sex."

That was the first thing John Schaefer ever said to Joseph. He had whizzed by on Joseph's first day in the hallway, his chair so close that Joseph had flinched. That had been Joseph's first real day in the chair, feeling the rubber tires under his hands. His fingers had blistered. He had stared down the hall at the back of John's head and watched as John wheeled about and rolled to a perfect stop in front of Joseph.

"You can. Swear to God. You might need to be a little creative, but that's a good thing."

That smile. The easy way he stroked the rubber of his tires, as if he were petting a cat.

"How do I know? Personal experience, my friend."

Then he had nodded at Joseph's fingers.

"Also, you might want to get yourself some gloves."

John Schaefer was probably whizzing away right now, back in the rehab unit. He had seemed never to sleep. Maybe another sixteen-year-old boy was there, a new para, venturing out in his chair for the first time. Maybe John Schaefer was telling him, right at this moment, that he could still have sex, that he just needed to be a little creative. But what if you had never had sex?

Three

"Don't think you can get away from me," Enzo said. "Because you can't."

She was waiting for him at the Dunn Brothers Coffee at 34th and Hennepin. It was morning, before his bakery shift, the time when Joseph usually pushed himself around the lake. "Work that upper body," John Schaefer had said. "That's what you've got left, so work it."

Enzo raised her clickster and pointed it at Joseph.

"I am everywhere," she said in the voice of an old horror-movie villain. "I know your every move."

Summer mornings were long in this northern land of no mountains and no ocean. With Enzo beside him, Joseph pushed himself down Hennepin to 34th and then right on 34th to the dead end on the little bluff above Lake Calhoun.

He gripped the tires tightly, halting down the sidewalk, over the leaves—trees thrusting their roots through cement—to the pedestrian crosswalk with the stop sign that most drivers only slowed for.

"Aren't you going to ask what I'm doing out so early?" Enzo said. "Aren't you going to ask if my mother knows where I am?"

Joseph shook his head.

"Just as I thought," Enzo said. She wiggled her clickster in the air as if signaling to an unknown observer that her prediction had come true. The lake shimmered in the sun. Joseph rolled down the path, and Enzo trotted beside him. The tall woman who walked her small black dog every morning was out. She nodded to Joseph and he nodded back. That was their routine. It was midmorning; the dew that silvered the grass overnight had dried, and gulls cried above.

Two narrow concrete paths circled the lake, separated by a few feet or a hundred yards at the far southern end. One path was for walkers and runners, the other for Rollerblades and bikers. A wheelchair was wheeled, but it belonged on the walking path; a wheelchair existed between worlds, neither here nor there.

"Where are we going?" Enzo said.

"Around," Joseph said.

They neared the 32nd Street playground. Enzo held her clickster loosely between thumb and forefinger as she walked, and undulated it up and down, so that it looked as if it were made of rubber. This was one of her favorite tricks.

To the far right of the playground was the children's wading pool. A sign at the far end informed parents that they should never leave their children unattended, never let their children swim naked. NO LIFEGUARD ON DUTY the sign read. NO SPITTING. NO RUNNING. NO DIVING.

After Labor Day, this children's wading pool would be drained. It would be revealed for what it was: a concrete circle dug into the sand, painted bright blue and filled from a garden hose. That was the way of children's wading pools; that was the way it had been at the Addison Miller playground in upstate New York.

The Erie Canal in upstate New York had been a shallow road made of water. The Hudson River began as a creek and surged its way south to the Atlantic. Here in Minneapolis, the Mississippi had a thousand miles to go before it emptied into the Gulf of Mexico. At its deepest, this children's wading pool was two feet deep, and at its deepest, Lake Calhoun was ninety feet deep, and at its deepest, the sea was miles deep. And that was it for the water of this earth; no matter how deep, deepness was measurable and finite.

"There's the little dude," Enzo said.

She pointed the clickster at a boy with black straight hair and the darkest of dark eyes. He was slender even for his small size, and he wore a black T-shirt with a bright green shamrock that read IRELAND ROCKS. The boy stood motionless at the top of the playground pirate ship lookout.

"The little dude goes to my school, you know," Enzo said. "His name is Cha. He's in the special classes."

The boy's fingers touched lightly on the bright red spokes of the pirate ship's rudder. Children clustered at the bottom of the pirate ship, looking up. They knew the child was not of them, and they did not know what he was.

"Don't stare," Enzo said in the voice of a lecturing grown-up. "It's not polite."

Cha gazed down from his pirate ship lookout across the small sand playground with its red and blue and green and yellow resin bouncing animals, and slides, and construction toys bolted into the ground.

"He's the captain of the ship," Joseph said.

"No he's not. He's the little dude. There are only eight kids like him in the whole world."

Cha stood at the top of the pirate's nest, on the pirate ship, at the pirate playground, and he gazed out to sea, the sea of Lake Calhoun.

"Ever heard of chromosomes?" Enzo said. "His are all messed up."

The child turned his head. Someone was calling his name.

"Cha," a girl sang softly. She was a girl with longer-than-long black hair. "Cha."

"That's his sister Mai," Enzo said. "She takes care of him. Nobody can remember the name of the thing he has. Nobody can keep it straight. It's too long."

A bee hovered around Enzo's face and she shied away, crouching like a scared toddler behind the back panel of Joseph's chair until the bee flew away.

"We just call him the little dude with the freaky chromosomes," Enzo said.

"Cha-a."

The girl named Mai's voice crooned again. She sat on a bench on the far side of the playground. A book lay face-down and open next to her. The bench was on springs, and Mai braced one toe against the sand and pushed off, so that the whole bench moved gently, like a baby's windup swing.

"Time to go," she said.

Mai was about Joseph's age. She must have felt Joseph looking at her, and she turned and looked back at him with no expression; she was a girl contained within herself.

"Cha," she said again, and she got up from the rocking bench. "It's time."

He frowned and made a sharp horizontal motion in the air with his hand.

"We'll be back," she said.

Her veil of black hair swung over her face, and she walked through the sand to the child and held her hand up to him. Joseph and Enzo watched them leave. Three pudgy toddlers who had been clustered at the base of the pirate ship rolled and tumbled their way up the gangplank and took Cha's place. Their high-pitched voices floated over the sand, over the bright resin animals, as they squabbled over who would hold the rudder now that the pirate captain was gone.

"You like the little dude," Enzo said.

She flipped her clickster back and forth from one hand to the other. Joseph had a vision of her catching it too hard, and the lead entering her palm, and he stopped himself from reaching out and grabbing the clickster mid-flip.

"Don't you?" Enzo said.

"I don't know him," Joseph said.

Flip. Flip. Flip. Joseph's eyes were on the lead, extended and sharp, ready to embed itself in Enzo's palm, a miniature black bullet.

"Maybe your chromosomes are freaky, too," Enzo said. "Ever think of that?"

Flip.

"Stop," Joseph said.

"Stop what? The clickster?" Enzo said. "I'm not scared of hurting myself."

A bee landed on Joseph's hand and Enzo cringed. Joseph kept his hand motionless. The bee lowered its back end toward the knuckle of his index finger, then lifted it again. Joseph could feel Enzo resisting the urge to run. Did the bee sense sweetness on Joseph's hand? Was skin sweet? The bee turned its body, clumsy when not suspended in air, around and around on the back of Joseph's hand. Enzo's body was clenched tight. She was held in thrall, ready to fight or flee if attacked. The bee gathered its heavy body and lifted itself into the air and droned away.

"Have you ever heard the creepy bird at Lake of the Isles?" Enzo said.

She lifted her head and shut her eyes and trilled out an unearthly wail.

"It's way worse than the little dude with the freaky chromosomes," she said. "It's worse than Kilt Man even. I wish that bird was dead."

The clickster stayed steady between her second and third fingers and Enzo nodded. Her eyes were steady on Joseph's.

"There are too many freaky people and birds in the world," she said. "I hate them all."

"It's a loon," Joseph said.

She waited, her eyes unblinking. She could hold her eyes

open without blinking longer than other people. Enzo nodded and kept her eyes fixed on Joseph's, as if she was sending him an unspoken signal. He sensed what she was waiting for and he beat her to it.

"No."

"No what?"

"No, I'm not a superhero."

"Yes you are," Enzo said in her controlled yell.

Now the feral children whipped down the pedestrian path on their bikes. The feral children were silent. The feral children were breaking the walker versus wheeled path rules. They hunched over their handlebars, feet pedaling furiously, heads down and hair flying behind them. They often flew by the bakery on missions unknown. If forced to by packs of pedestrians, the feral children would burst onto Hennepin Avenue itself, causing cars to screech and honk, but they preferred the sidewalks. If the way was blocked by only a single pedestrian, the stream of feral children would split as if in a predetermined pattern and flow around the walker, who would abruptly halt, terrorized into silence by sudden ambush.

"And those bike kids," Enzo said. "I hate them, too."

"Why?"

"Why do you think? They're freaky."

Standing, she hunched in midair, her hands held out like claws gripping invisible handlebars. The feral children came whipping back down the path. They looked neither left nor right, and they made no sound but the whirring blur of their pedals and wheels.

"I bet you can't go that fast in that wheelchair of yours, can you?"

"No."

"Why don't you get an electric one, then? If you had an electric wheelchair you could go faster than them."

"No I couldn't."

"On hills you could."

"There are no hills here."

"Maybe not hills like where you're from, in beekeeper world," Enzo said. "Whatever world that is, which I don't know anything about because you won't cooperate with my investigation."

Her voice rose. Joseph was silent. The angry child was sparking and ready for a fight. The feral children whipped past again. One of them was carrying a stick in one hand. They were circling, on the lookout for what, Joseph didn't know.

Click. Another bit of lead extruded itself from the clickster.

"Tell me how your legs got hurt."

"They don't hurt. They're paralyzed, remember?"

Click.

"Fine. If you won't tell me, then I'll tell you. Don't think I don't know what really happened."

Joseph closed his eyes.

"Everybody thinks your legs got hurt because Zap told them you fell off the precipice," Enzo said. "You were risking life and limb to rescue your mother from a fate worse than death and you fell."

Joseph opened his eyes and saw that the child's eyes were again too bright.

"But what nobody knows is that then you stopped falling," Enzo whispered. "That's the secret. You stopped falling and you flew through thin air. You flew through the clouds and the sun and you are the only person in the history of the world to fly without wings."

"No."

"Yes."

He saw that no matter what he said, she would match him word for word, so great was her desire. It was past time to put an end to this, and yet the child would not listen.

"If what you say is true," Joseph said, "then why did I break my back when I landed? Why can't I just get up and walk right now?"

She was already shaking her head in anticipation of his denials, forbidding him any rebuttal. Logic had no place in Enzo world.

"You can," she said. "You just don't want to."

Her clickster was pointed directly at him.

"Don't worry, I won't tell anyone," she said. "Superheroes can't talk about their past. Everyone knows that."

"Enzo—"

"Mighty Thor."

"Listen to me. I don't want to have to keep saying this."

"Don't say you're not a superhero," Enzo said in her controlled yell. It came out of nowhere. She swarmed at will, turning upon herself. Joseph looked at her, at her bright and burning eyes.

"You're the beekeeper from the island of bees," she said. "And you flew through the sun and the clouds and you landed on the deep blue sea."

The lead of the clickster was too long, too exposed. It would break soon.

"Please be a superhero," Enzo said. "Please."

Her voice was hushed. Joseph's fingers wanted to be on the rubber of his tires, pushing, shoving. The glide and hush of his wheels on the pavement, faster than a small girl could keep up. Faster than a small girl could run.

Shove.

Glide.

Everything was bigger in the Midwest. The houses and apartment buildings were bigger. The roads were wider. The people were bigger and the cars were bigger. No mountains broke up the horizon, no narrow valleys to hide in. The Old Erie Canal trail back home in upstate New York was narrow, carved out more than a century ago by men and their beasts of burden. Men had contained water and used it for their own purposes, their flat-bottomed barges lighter in the water than on the land.

Once, Joseph had biked from Utica to Rome on the canal trail, and then biked on, his shadow stretching yards ahead of him, toward the west. If he had kept on biking, he would have ended up here, in this land of wide boulevards and gridlike streets that ran perfectly north and south and east and west.

On that day on the Old Erie Canalway, Joseph could not have imagined that this wide Midwest was where he would find himself.

On that biking day in upstate New York, the trail stretching ahead of him, mountains to the north, Joseph would have said no to this future.

No to the wheelchair.

No to the flatlands.

No to Lake Calhoun in the morning, water contained within a shallow bowl of land. No to the walkers swinging their arms like metronomes, and the dogs trotting on their leashes, and the seagulls crying and circling overhead. Didn't they know they were seagulls, meant to live on the sea?

"Stop going so fast," Enzo said.

She was panting. Her feet slapped the ground behind him. How could they be so stupid, these gulls, thinking that a lake three miles in circumference contained the mysteries of the ocean? They knew nothing. These inland gulls were freaks of their species, with no sense of the tides that tugged at the great waters of the world, that pushed and pulled with the moon.

"I said stop! Why do you always have to go so fast?"

They had made it as far as the bridge that spanned the narrow walled channel between Lake Calhoun and Lake of the Isles. Adults passed by and gazed with curiosity—a boy in a chair, an angry child—and then averted their eyes. Joseph's hands on the tires were hot, the skin puffed and red. He had forgotten his gloves. Joseph looked at the child in front of him. She was close to tears.

"What are you doing out so early?" he said. "Does your mother know where you are?"

" 'What are you doing out so early?' " she mimicked in a high adult voice. Her too-bright eyes bored into him. " 'Does your mother know where you are?' "

"Go home. Your mother needs you."

"No, *you* go home. Your mother's the one who needs you."

Enzo began to back away from him on the narrow path of the bridge, heedless of the bikes and blades that might be swooping up behind her. Sunlight coaxed the hidden red from her head of springy dark curls.

"She's in the hospital," she said. "Did you forget that?"

"Stop it."

"Don't you think you should go get her, Mr. Superhero? Fly away home."

It came clawing up inside him again, swarming through his lungs and his chest and his shoulders and then down his arms. No matter how hard he worked, shoving himself around the lake every morning and swimming himself to oblivion every night, he could not keep the buzzing panic at bay. It had come to pass that his mother was in the hospital. Despite all the months, years even, of listening and attending and taking care, what he most dreaded had happened. And what had happened to their apartment, and the Scrabble board permanently set up on the kitchen table? And the dark winter coat, was that hanging somewhere in the hospital, waiting for her? Joseph had closed his eyes into darkness and opened them into this unfamiliar geography, this large, flat Midwest. It seemed impossible that Joseph's mother should be in this world, living and breathing, and that he himself should be in this same world, this same world of plains and mountains and rivers and clouds, and yet he could not reach her.

Now Enzo hunched before him with a look of fear, her shoulders curved over as if she were trying to protect herself. Why was she standing that way? The air around them was still. But Joseph's breath came hard. Had he been shouting? Had he been pounding his legs with his fists?

He set his hands on the tires. The rubber was warm.

You stopped falling and you flew through thin air. You flew through the clouds and the sun. Now she turned and ran. When she reached the Tin Fish Café, she turned back and faced him and cupped her hands around her mouth. The cry came trilling high and floated down the block to where Joseph sat suspended on the small bridge over the channel, curved over his own chest in the chair. The creepy bird, the cry of a loon: Enzo's farewell.

Four

"Welcome to the bakery," Zap said, speaking into a baguette as if he were a radio announcer and the baguette were a microphone. "Where the men are good-looking, the women are strong, and the children are welcome. With the exception of one named Enzo."

A long piece of bakery string dangled from his other hand, wiggling like bait. Joseph was the fish. Enzo had not yet arrived; Zap's idiot-child walls had not yet been built for the day. His long braids swung forward over his tanned face, and his eyes were unnaturally blue in the sun streaming through the window.

"And who have we here with us in the bakery today?" Zap intoned. "Why, it is Joseph, known to most of you listeners out there as the beekeeper from the island of bees."

Once, Joseph had seen Zap with his hair loose and un-braided. It was wild hair, hair of honey and gold and brown, hair that wanted to play. Sometimes he wove feathers or strands of grass into his braids, or tiny items designed to amuse the children who loved him. Not today.

"We're lucky to have Joseph with us today," Zap said. "It's not every beekeeper who tumbles from a precipice into the rock-strewn surf and lives to tell the tale."

Joseph took the bakery string and gazed up at Zap, who had put down the baguette and was leaning over the counter, a pair of tiny glasses encrusted with sparkling fake gems dangling from his fingers. He put them on and squinted at Joseph.

"You like them?" Zap said. "Reading glasses. One dollar at the Dollar Store on Nicollet."

"I thought reading glasses were only for old people."

"They are. Do you like them?"

Joseph studied the miniature glasses. The fake gems flashed in the sunlight.

"The keeper of bees likes the reading glasses," Zap said in his radio announcer's voice. "And who can blame him? He is drawn to the magnificent jewels."

Zap crouched next to Joseph's wheelchair and studied its wheels, which were narrow and sinewy and tilted slightly inward.

"What do you think of this wheelchair?" Zap said. "Big was freaked about what kind to get for you."

Big's back appeared in the air before Joseph, the back of a man, bent and curving over the radiator by the window of Joseph's room in rehab. A blue cotton shirt untucked over

baggy pants that needed a belt. Here and there on the forearms of this bent man were dark spots: burns. Joseph had lain
in his bed and watched the back of this man, counted the
burns on each forearm, until the bent man turned around.

"Hey," Big had said, and Joseph had nodded.

"Joseph," Big had said, and come toward him with his
hands out. "Your mother——"

"Don't talk about my mother to me," Joseph said.

Big had been a mixer in the bakery in Utica, before he'd
left Joseph and his mother. The Utica bakery had baked Italian bread, fifteen different kinds: ciabatta, Italian rolls, focac-
cia, pizza shells. Mixer was a big step up from oven guy. Two
hundred and fifty pounds of flour at a time. But here in Minneapolis Big was an oven guy. Big's back, bent over the sink
when he got home, burned hands cupped under the faucet to
splash away the flour, shade in his bedroom drawn down and
duct-taped to the sill to keep out the sun.

Big's head was bent and he looked up at Joseph through
dark eyes, like a child who had done something wrong.

"Don't ever talk about her," Joseph said, and Big nodded.

Joseph would go with Big because he had to, he would go
away from the streets of Utica, where he ran at dawn every
day, he would leave behind the mountains and the familiar
names and the kitchen with its pale green walls, where the
Scrabble game lay unfinished, but he would not talk.

"Earth to Joseph," Zap said. "Earth to Flying Joseph."

He waved his hand in front of Joseph's face.

"Big asked the Figurehead about wheelchairs," he said,
"like the Figurehead would have any clue. In the end, he got
hold of some spinal-cord woman at Sister Kenny."

Big rose after Joseph had gone to work. Sometimes he and
his friends walked by the bakery on their way to Liquor
Lyle's. Liquor Lyle's had no windows. It was impossible to see
through the yellow brick walls and take note of Big and his
friends. Maybe they sat in Liquor Lyle's drinking. Maybe they
played cards. Maybe they didn't. Maybe they told stories.
Maybe they didn't. Maybe they talked about boys in wheelchairs. Maybe they talked about one boy in one wheelchair,
the boy who had journeyed across the country to live with his
father. How did the boy go to the bathroom? Would the boy
ever walk again? Could the boy still have sex? Maybe Big and
his friends talked about things like that inside the windowless
walls of Liquor Lyle's. Maybe they didn't.

"Big put the time in," Zap said. "He did the research. I'll
give him that."

"I used to run," Joseph said. "I used to bike."

Behind the jeweled reading glasses, Zap's eyes darkened
and squinted.

"You used to run," he repeated. He ran his hand up and
down the wheel and pinched the tire as if it were a bike tire,
possibly in need of air. "You used to bike. Like, a lot?"

Tiredness washed through Joseph and he wanted Zap's
hands off his wheels. Deep within the skin, below the wasted
muscle, inside the bones that were still doing their work of
marrow and iron, Joseph's legs wanted to move. His brain sent
out the commands: Rise, run. Rise, run. But no matter how
much Joseph willed his legs to comprehend, they could make
no sense of the sent impulses. He saw himself back home, running past the darkened storefronts of dawn in upstate New
York. His gaze was fixed on the foothills, pushing north to-

ward the high peaks, north toward the purple cloud-shrouded shoulders of the Adirondacks, shrugging their way down the spine of upstate New York.

"Is it all mountains out there?"

Zap spoke of the Northeast as if it were a foreign country, a land existing out of time and space. Joseph nodded. Mountains.

"None here," Zap offered.

Zap turned back to the stack of chocolate-chip cookies he was breaking into tiny paper cups for Batman and Windbreaker Boy and the other children in his flock. Joseph gathered his long hair in one hand and wrapped the string around it with the other and tied a slipknot by feel. Then he rolled to the lemonade and picked up one of the plastic cups of fresh-squeezed lemonade that rested there on the bed of ice. The bees craved sugar. Time to feed the bees.

"Excuse me?"

It was Mai, the girl from the playground. No small Cha in an IRELAND ROCKS T-shirt next to her, holding her hand, on which trembled a bracelet of many-colored beads. Joseph focused on the bracelet. A tiny knot kept each bead from its neighbor. Had someone sat and squinted and tied each of those knots by hand?

Mai pointed at the double-fudge brownies.

"How much are those?"

"It's after five," Joseph said. "So they're half off."

She waited. He waited.

"So . . ."

"Oh, sorry. Fifty cents. Now. Since it's after five."

"Okay. I'll take one."

Joseph plucked up the best one, one with no corners, one from the center of the pan. The bakery case was too high for him to pass it over, so Joseph rolled to the cash register and handed it to her, tucked in a square of bakery tissue. Mai gave him two quarters, and he opened the register and placed them in the quarter compartment. She sat at a table by the window and nibbled.

Was it time for Joseph to go to the bathroom? Did he have to go? Should he go just in case he had to go and didn't know it? Was he leaking onto the floor? Was there a puddle of pee beneath his chair, and if he looked down, would he see it, and would Zap then look down and see it, too, and would Mai then look down? Joseph did not look down.

Snap.

"Flying Joseph."

Zap snapped his fingers again under Joseph's nose. Zap's fingers smelled of lemon and frosting. His hair smelled dry and warm and heavy, the way weeds and Queen Anne's lace and milkweed smelled by the side of the road in upstate New York in the late summer, when Joseph had run north out of the city, past the wetlands, into the countryside.

Joseph willed himself not to look down at the floor beneath his chair, but he looked down.

No puddle.

"Flying Joseph."

Zap's fingers hovered under Joseph's nose, ready to snap again, ready to call Joseph back to the tray of lemon squares before him, back to the stack of white paper doilies that fluttered in the breeze from the open doors. Back to the room of many windows, where people sat at round wooden tables and drank iced coffee and talked and laughed and gazed out at a Minneapolis summer under the tall green canopies of oaks and elms.

"What did you just call him?" Mai said.

"His name," Zap said.

"Flying Joseph is not a name."

"In my world it is," Zap said. "But perhaps you do not live in my world. Perhaps you live in a world of little imagination."

The girl lifted her chin and gave Zap a look.

"Nice glasses," she said.

"Why, thank you."

Zap tilted his head so that the bejeweled reading glasses slid down his nose. The beads of the girl's bracelet sparkled in the sun. They shimmered and trembled on the translucent string that held them together and apart. The beads were in a prison hospital, highly medicated, and they could not stand on their own. They needed the knots that separated them in order to keep them upright. Without those knots, the beads would stumble and fall. Maybe they wanted to fall. Maybe they wanted to sleep. But they were held upright and upright they would remain.

"Flying Joseph," Zap sang. "Come back, Flying Joseph."

He crouched, crooning next to Joseph's face. The bracelet and its medicated beads receded. The lemon squares sat dully on their tray in a patch of sunlight on Joseph's table. The bakery made too many lemon squares. They never sold them all, even at half-off time. Confectioners' sugar had been sprinkled with a generous hand, and the shortbread pastry on the bottom was thick. So was the lemon filling.

Joseph's mother liked lemon squares. She liked Parker House rolls with butter. She liked saltines with peanut butter spread over the top, spread all the way to the edges, thin and smooth. Sometimes she played Scrabble by a reward system: Less than ten points and she could have a single bite of saltine, greater than ten but less than twenty and she could eat the entire saltine, anything over thirty and the lemon square was hers. Joseph looked at the lemon squares in their precise rows on the platter.

"Don't you want to know why I call him Flying Joseph?" Zap said.

"Not really," Mai said.

"But it's an interesting story," Zap said, "one that our radio listeners have been waiting to hear, as well."

He plucked a caramel from the bowl of Auntie Apple's wax paper–wrapped caramels on the counter and unwrapped it. He flipped it up into the air and leaped and caught it in his mouth. Zap was a Frisbee-catching dog in training. Zap the Frisbee dog gulped down the caramel and reached for another, and another. Zap the Frisbee dog caught the Frisbee three times in a row and Zap the Frisbee dog was delighted with himself and did a little caramel victory dance. His braids jumped and swayed.

"The boy before you," Zap said, "is one of the few people in the history of the world to fly wingless through thin air and live to tell the tale."

Mai raised her eyebrows.

"The boy who fell to Earth and survived," Zap said in his radio announcer's voice. "That's why we call him Flying

Joseph. Some even call him a hero. But not the boy himself. The boy himself is too humble to use the word *hero*."

"Does everyone in your world have a nickname?" Mai said.

"Everyone except you. You shall be known as the Lovely One."

Mai flushed, but her gaze held steady. "That right there is a nickname."

"No it's not. It's merely the truth."

Zap could say things like that. They came right out of his mouth and he didn't blush, and Mai laughed, and that was the way it was in Zap world. Everyone who entered was at ease, unless her name was Enzo and she was nine years old and carried a clickster like a weapon at her side.

Mai took a small bite of her double-fudge brownie. Zap pushed his reading glasses back up his nose and regarded her.

"O Lovely One," he said, "since the subject has been broached, what would you say is the essential quality of a superhero?"

She nibbled her brownie and nudged her shoulders up and down, the tiniest of I-don't-knows.

"It's a serious question," Zap said. "It's the question of the day, here at the bakery. No tights. No capes. No clinging to buildings with web-spinning palms. What sets the superhero apart? What makes him stand out from the crowd?"

"Superheroes aren't supposed to stand out from the crowd," Mai said. "The superhero is only a superhero anonymously. No one in the ordinary world ever knows who he is."

"Or she," Zap said.

Now Joseph had to go. Did he have to go? It was time. He

must have to go. He wheeled himself past the door that led to the back room, and beyond that to the bakery itself, and beyond that to the ovens, where in eight hours Big would be standing, and with difficulty made his way into the unisex rest room.

"He had a girlfriend," Big said. "Back in Utica."

Zap gave Joseph a warning look as he emerged from the back door into the bakery, a look that said, Big and his short friend are here and they have been drinking. Mai was gone, and Big and his short friend were standing on either side of Zap in the bakery. How long had they been there? How long had Joseph been in the rest room?

"Sure he did," the short friend said. This was the friend who nodded vigorously at everything Big said.

"Her name was Anne," Big said. "Or Anna. Annie, maybe. She was there at the hospital. Pretty."

The short friend nodded, and Big nodded, too. Big's voice was loud. He was ready and willing to take on the challengers, those who would argue with him that Joseph did not have a girlfriend, that the girlfriend had not been at the hospital and was not pretty. Big twisted his Saranac cap in his hands, the cap he had bought from the Utica Club Brewery back in upstate New York, back when he still lived with Joseph and Joseph's mother. Big was tall, but when you looked closely, he was not as tall as the name Big would signify, and he was thin, not fat. Joseph did not look closely. He brushed his eyes in the general direction of Big: blue work shirt, baggy work pants,

Saranac beer cap twisted between both hands. Big did not look at Joseph, either.

"Pretty," Big said again.

"Hey, big guy," Zap said. "Why don't you talk a little louder there?"

Zap looked right at Big and tilted his head a little, as if he were a teacher being sarcastic with a student. Big stood still and looked at Zap. His big body was dull around the edges, his clothes drooping over the slopes and valleys of his shoulders and stomach and hips. He was trying to gather himself, Joseph saw, trying to gather himself and figure out who Zap was and what he was doing behind the counter with his braids and his wide eyes and his words that held no fear.

"Isn't that Frank's kid?" the short friend said.

"Yeah."

Big nodded again. Here was a way out. Here was a way to leave the bakery. This was the boss's kid. The boss's kid could not be confronted.

"Well. Fuck."

"Yeah. Fuck."

They passed down the sidewalk, the tall one and the short one. Big did not look back. Zap picked three lemons out of the bowl by the iced tea and tossed them—flip, flip, flip—into the air, the middle lemon jumping higher than the others with each round of juggling.

"So, Flying Joseph," Zap said. "I hear you had a girlfriend."

He looked at Joseph, still juggling.

"And she was pretty, goddamn it," he said in Big's voice. "You hear me? She was pretty."

Then he caught each lemon and laid them gently on the wooden cutting board.

"Mai has a crush on you," Zap said.

His paring knife sliced each lemon into thin wedges and his nimble fingers piled them into a small green bowl, ready for the tea drinkers.

"What?" Zap said. "Don't give me that look. It's obvious, man. Let me ask you something, flyboy. You had a girlfriend since you been in that chair?"

Joseph shook his head.

"I figured," Zap said. "But here's the thing: It's the same as usual. You just have to adjust a few things. Like, she has to tip her head upside down to kiss you."

Three more lemons from the lemon bowl. One lemon flying, and now two lemons flying, and now a third lemon under the leg and straight up.

"I've been pondering the situation, as it were," Zap said. "And it shouldn't be a problem."

There. Zap had said what he needed to say. The path was smooth now, in the world according to Zap, for Flying Joseph and all future girlfriends. Tip your head upside down and all would be well.

Kilt Man stood in his appointed position outside the far window, long slanting rays of sun falling over him. Today his muttering was audible, a stream of language that Joseph willed himself not to hear. The Kilt Men of the earth were legion. They walked the streets, gazing into worlds not their own.

Once, it had seemed to Joseph that if only he listened closely enough, he would be able to understand. Once, Joseph had listened and listened, and in his listening he had sensed that sense was being made, but the sense belonged to a distant world, a world below the surface, a world of seawater and boulder-strewn sand.

"No eggs today, my kilted friend," Zap called. "I'll boil you some up tomorrow, though."

Kilt Man ignored him, as he always did. Today he wore a coil of tinfoil around his neck.

"That's a nice necklace you have there," Zap said. "Did you make it?"

Kilt Man ignored him. Did he hear Zap? Did he hear anyone? Now he walked away. Zap tossed a caramel into the air and caught it.

"Kilt Man has left the building," he said in his radio announcer's voice. "Will Kilt Man return? Tune in again tomorrow and find out."

Joseph gathered up his hair, which had slipped out of the bakery-string tie, and tied it again. It would not last. His hair was long, and it slid over his shoulders, and when it was wet from the pool it cooled him through the long hot Minneapolis nights.

"Some of you out there may be wondering if Kilt Man has the essential quality of a superhero," Zap said. "We are sorry to report that no, he does not."

Zap tossed two caramels into the air and caught them both. Toss. Catch.

"Why not, you ask? Too schizo. Too egg-oriented."

Joseph pushed himself to the end of the counter and began to roll plastic knives and forks and spoons into napkins, ready for tomorrow's picnickers.

"What shall we tell people when they ask about your legs,

Flying Joseph?" Zap said. "We should come up with a party line of some kind."

"Tell them the truth. That I fell."

"Don't you want to make it a better story than that?"

Joseph concentrated on the task at hand. Knife, fork, spoon, napkin: Roll.

"Like a tree, maybe. A tree that out of the blue fell on you when you were out running in those mountains of yours out there, out east, out wherever you came from."

Knife, fork, spoon, napkin: Roll.

"Or you were skydiving and the parachute didn't open, but you landed on a pile of mattresses that had just at that moment fallen off the back of a semi and you miraculously survived."

Knife, fork, spoon, napkin: Roll.

"Or you took a bullet to the back in a drive-by shooting."

Knife, fork, spoon, napkin: Roll.

"Or I fell," Joseph said.

Zap regarded Joseph through his reading glasses, which had again slipped down his nose. The reading glasses winked and sparkled—snow turned diamond by sun.

"So that's your story," Zap said. "That's your story and you're sticking to it."

"It's not a story; it's the truth."

Zap looked at Joseph's legs, studying them as if this information had somehow changed their appearance.

"The truth is never simple, Flying Joseph," Zap said. "When did this fall take place?"

"Last winter. January."

"And where?"

"In upstate New York, in the Addison Miller playground pool."

"A pool in January. Empty?"

"Filled with snow."

"Dirty old or fresh white?"

Zap asked the question as if it mattered, as if it was important that he be able to picture the fallen Joseph in a pool covered with snow back in Utica, New York, and he needed the details to be right.

"Fresh white," Joseph said.

"Did you know right away that you were paralyzed?"

The snow had been cold, frozen powder against his cheek. The sun was piercing and Joseph had kept opening his eyes and then closing them. There had been many voices and then sirens.

"I don't remember," Joseph said. "I kept trying to get up."

He had kept trying to get up. There was something he needed to do. There was someplace he needed to be. It was urgent. He had kept trying to get up, but his legs wouldn't move. Then he had been lifted and strapped onto a board.

Zap tossed another caramel in the air, so high that it zinged off the pressed-tin ceiling and rebounded off a bakery case.

"And how did you come to fall?"

Joseph shook his head.

"Why does the boy fall?" Zap said in his announcer's voice. "We know not. What we know is that the boy falls, and in the falling almost dies."

"I didn't almost die."

"Let the record show that we have called a reluctant witness to the stand."

"It's the truth."

"You're in a wheelchair, aren't you? Close enough." Zap resumed his announcer's voice. "And the moment the boy was paralyzed for life was the moment when his superpower came into being."

"I didn't almost die, I am not a superhero, and I have no superpower."

Zap made a face and flicked his fingers in the air as if he were ridding himself of a dead spider. Details. He picked up a bakery chair and began hoisting it up and down above his head. He was constantly at work on his shoulders and biceps. It was his belief that women loved broad shoulders and big biceps.

"You *are* paralyzed for life, aren't you?" Zap said.

They both looked at Joseph's legs in their faded jeans.

"Okay, great," Zap said. "Paralyzed for life."

Five

Enzo was waiting for Joseph at the bakery, sitting cross-legged on the sidewalk. She would no longer go inside unless Joseph was there.

"It's 1:09," she announced. "You're late. You're late for a very important date."

"Hello to you too, Enzo."

"Mighty Thor," she said.

Enzo tapped at the heavy man's watch on her wrist. Enzo liked to know time to the minute. Joseph had watched her in the bakery more than once, Enzo intent on the slow sweep of the second hand on the clock that hung on the wall above the coffee station. "It's 11:11," she would announce. "God will appear." It was her belief that four ones equaled the opportunity for a miracle. She had told Joseph that her parents prayed a lot.

"Isn't that Zap's watch?" Joseph said.

"No. This watch is a watch that I found on the sidewalk."

"It looks like Zap's watch to me."

"Well it's not. It's my watch."

She clicked her clickster. She clicked it again.

"You're wasting lead," Joseph said.

Click. Click. Click click clickclickclick. The clickster was furious, chittering away with much to say. The lead grew steadily, until the entire slender shaft dropped out of the barrel.

"Now see what you did, idiot child," Enzo said in a high, scolding imitation of an adult voice.

She held down the tip of the clickster with her thumb and carefully slid the long line of lead back into the barrel. She released her thumb and the lead stayed.

"What would you do if I weren't here to clean up your messes, idiot child?" Enzo said in the same scolding voice. "Praise the Lord that you have a mother."

"Does the Mighty Thor believe in God?" Joseph said.

"The Mighty Thor believes in freaky chromosomes."

Enzo pointed the nervous clickster at his legs.

"If I were a superhero, my legs wouldn't be hurt."

"My legs don't hurt."

"You're doing it again," Enzo said in her controlled yell. "You never answer me."

Her man's watch slipped down her wrist and halfway over her clenched fist. She was in danger of losing it. Joseph rolled over the slight hump of the doorsill and into the bakery, and Enzo followed him. Zap bent over the day-old racks, bagging yesterday's bread for the silent food-shelf man. Enzo went to her table and lined up her clickster exactly parallel with the salt and pepper shakers.

"Don't you want to know what the very important date is?" she said. Enzo gazed at Joseph, her eyes boring into his. "Read my mind and tell me what it is. Very . . . important . . . date."

"I can't."

"You can," she whispered. "You just don't want to admit it."

Click. She sat back in her brown velvet chair as if a test had been completed.

"So," she said. "Do you miss it?"

"Do I miss what?"

"Your home. That place back there in the mountains, the island of bees, wherever it is you came from."

Joseph tied his hair back with a rubber band from the box they kept on the counter. It would hurt later, when he pulled it off that night. He knew this, but he rubber-banded his hair anyway, into a ponytail tighter than usual. Enzo pointed the clickster at his legs.

"People like you are supposed to fix things that are hurt," she said.

"I'm a failure, then."

"Superheroes don't fail."

Enzo's voice was tight. Tendrils of anger were beginning to unfurl within her. And Joseph was angering, too. His mother stood in the kitchen before the rain-blotched window and smiled. He watched from the doorway. Her dark winter coat was dirty, but she would not wash it; if she washed it, the coat would no longer keep her warm. Her hands worried themselves together, small chapped fingers climbing one over another. She was in the kitchen with the pale green walls and the unwashed window, and Joseph stood in the doorway, and how long could they remain like this? How long could he stand between her and the world outside?

"Hello," Enzo said. "Did you even hear me?"

"I heard you."

Joseph put his hands on his tires and shoved. The lemonades in their lidded cups waited on their bed of ice. The shallow bowls waited behind the counter, next to the stack of take-out containers. The bees were awake; it was time for the beekeeper to attend to his work. A quick tilt of the lemonade cup into a bowl, and then another quick tilt, and another, and then all the bowls lined up on a tray, and the tray balanced on Joseph's lap, and then hands to the tires again, and out into the room, the room of lemonadeless tables.

"Seen your new girlfriend today, Flying Joseph?" Zap said.

"What?" Enzo said. Her eyes moved back and forth from Zap to Joseph. "Who?"

"Flying Joseph's got a girlfriend. Don't tell me the investigator didn't know."

Click. "Who is it?"

"Mai."

"The freaky little dude's sister?"

"She likes his biceps," Zap said. "She likes his long hair."

Enzo pointed the clickster at Joseph.

"Is that true?" she demanded. "Do you like Mai?"

The empty tray sat on Joseph's lap. Anna Micciolini's face came to him. The last time Joseph had seen Anna Micciolini was in the hospital. Her face had been white. In the middle of chaos, Joseph had noticed that about her, her white and freck-leless face. Her quiet eyes in her white unfreckled face had gazed down at the floor, not at him.

"Girlfriends are stupid," Enzo said.

"Flying Joseph doesn't think so," Zap said.

"He should be thinking about his mother," Enzo said. "His mother back on the island of bees."

"Don't talk about his mother. You'll disappear him again."

Four brown grocery bags filled with day-old bread stood before Zap next to the cash register. He stood behind his fortress, only his head visible, eyes lasering into the back of Enzo's head. His braids were tied in back with a hank of mul-ticolored curling ribbon that looked as if it had been recycled from a child's birthday gift.

"The beer guy said you played Scrabble with your mother every day," Enzo said. "On that island of yours in the middle of the Adirondack sea. Which is full of rocks, by the way."

Enzo was off in her world of suppressed yells.

"Lake Calhoun doesn't have any rocks," she said. "That means it's better than your island. And guess what? Your mother's not the only one who knows how to play Scrabble, so ha-ha."

She moved to the side, so that Joseph had an unobstructed view of her table, where a Scrabble board was set up.

"This is your very important date. See? It turns. It's the deluxe version. Which I bet you didn't have back on that island."

She gave the board a spin. It clunked around in an awk-ward circle.

"You don't have it set up right," Joseph said.

He picked the board off the base and flipped the base upside down, then set the board back down and gave it another spin: smooth and swift. Enzo ignored him.

"The tiles have individual compartments," she said. "They don't fall out. They don't get shoved around. You don't have to worry that your words will get messed up. It's the deluxe version."

She held up a wine-colored bag.

"It comes with its own bag for the tiles," Enzo said. "That's because it's the deluxe version."

"Hey, beekeeper," Zap said. "Are you getting the impression that this Scrabble game is the deluxe version?"

"Shut up," Enzo said. She shook the bag again at Joseph. "So do you want to play?"

"I'll play," Joseph said.

"Are you any good?"

"Not as good as some people."

"Like your mother? The beer guy said she's good. I could beat her, though. Know how I know? Because the beer guy told the Figurehead that she was beyond reach."

Enzo shook the bag of letters. Inside the wine-colored fabric, invisible tiles leaped up and down, clattering against one another. When Joseph's mother played Scrabble, she bowed her head and touched her fingertips together and closed her eyes before she opened the bag. *Dear God of Scrabble, if you see fit to provide me with both a* Q *and a* U *at the same time, I promise to use the triple-word square to the best of my earthly ability.* She had not said that in a long time, but she used to say it before every turn.

Enzo closed her eyes and withdrew seven tiles. She

arranged them on her tile rack and frowned. She reached into the bag and withdrew more.

"You can only take seven tiles," Joseph said.

"I'm nine and you're sixteen. Therefore I get to take sixteen. It's called a handicap. Ever heard of it?"

Sixteen tiles was far too many for the tile rack. Letters spilled onto the table in front of Enzo and she moved them back and forth with her index finger, forming and re-forming words.

"What about Mighty Thor?" she said. "How many points would that be?"

"None," Joseph said. "Mighty Thor is two separate words, plus it's a proper name."

"Maybe in wheelchair world it is. But not in Enzo world."

Enzo upended the wine-colored bag and dumped all the tiles out onto her gouged table. Her fingers flicked through the letters, separating one and then another. Zap, who was taping enormous fake zinnias to the pens in the pen cup, came over to inspect.

"You can't pick and choose the letters you want," Zap said.

"In Enzo world you can."

Her fingers flicked six letters into a row: **S O O P E R.**

"That's not how you spell *super*," Zap said.

"It is in Enzo world, which is a way better world than Zap world."

"How so?"

"Because nobody named Zap lives in Enzo world. That's why."

Zap's fingers smoothed duct tape around another pen, binding the plastic orange zinnia to its slender shaft. He turned and walked away, back to the cash register, his back stiff and straight.

"Do you wish someone named Zap did live in Enzo world?" Joseph said to Enzo.

"No. Not one bit."

Her voice was bold, but she was sad, a sad child whose sadness shivered its way out to Joseph. Her fingers finished flicking through the tiles and **S O O P E R H E R O E** lay flat and defiant in the middle of the Scrabble board. Joseph wanted to put his hand on Enzo's, but he knew she would flinch away if he did. He reached out to the tiles and covered up the **S O O P E R H E R O E** with his palm. Be still, sooperheroe. Disappear into your sooperheroe world, wherever that world might be.

"I am going now," Enzo said. "Good-bye."

The Mighty Thor walked straight out the door and turned left without looking back. The Mighty Thor was only nine years old, but she was capable of not looking back.

The silent food-shelf man would be in at any moment. He would walk straight to the counter, where the bags were lined up. He would hoist two of them, one in each hand, and carry them by their handles to his car, parked outside. Then he would return for the other two bags. The silent food-shelf man would not look at Joseph in his chair, nor would he look at Zap and his ribboned hair.

"Mayday, Mayday," Zap said from the coffee urns. He was a police dispatcher, tense and focused. "A cream emergency has just been declared. All emergency vehicles, please respond."

They often ran out of cream at the bakery. Zap believed that coffee should be drunk black or with, at most, a tiny splash of skim milk. He disapproved of the amount of cream customers added to their coffee and the rate at which the half-and-half disappeared. The carafe of skim milk remained full, and the carafe of half-and-half was often empty, but in Zap world, the customer was not always right. In Zap world, the customer was often wrong. Zap always underordered the half-and-half.

Now he held up two quarts of half-and-half and shook them. Empty. He tossed them into the air and began to juggle.

"I'll go," Joseph said.

Beyond the open double doors, the long summer afternoon lay before him. The streets here were laid out in a perfect grid, right angles on a compass, unlike the Utica city streets that Joseph was used to. The end of each block here in uptown had a good sloping curb cut, good for wheelchairing. Joseph pulled on his black biking half gloves and rolled himself up and over the small hump of the doorsill.

"They are the exact kind of gloves that a wheelchair superhero would wear," Zap said. "Formfitting and mysterious in a could-be-sinister way."

Joseph put his gloved hands on the rubber of his tires and shoved.

"And that is exactly the way a wheelchair superhero would shove the tires."

Just past the giant oak, a dusty white sedan blocked the

curb cut. Uptown was a popular place. Maybe the driver had hesitated before parking here, in just this spot. Maybe he had believed there were no other parking spots nearby, and he would be there for only an hour or so, and the Calhoun Square lot was too expensive. The hell with it. Just this once, he would block the curb cut. How many wheelchairs were going to pass by here anyway?

The driver had nosed the car up so far that his front bumper nudged the car in front. There was no way around. Joseph rolled up onto the grass, but it had rained overnight and the grass was wet, and his tires spun in the mud.

"Asshole," Zap said. He was breathing hard. He must have been watching from the doorway and come running. "Or assholette. Women can be assholes, too. Hold tight."

Zap gripped the handles of the chair and then Joseph was tilting back a few inches, looking into the high leaves of the giant oak. *Thump.*

"Sorry," Zap said.

They were on the street.

"It's all right," Joseph said.

"The hell it is. Hang on."

Zap turned to the car, then back to Joseph. He held out a grimy forefinger as if it was contaminated. PIG had appeared in the dirt on the side of the car. Zap's anger was shimmering up again, the way it did sometimes, a boulder in the ocean, covered and then revealed by the outgoing tide.

"The world is full of lazy shits," Zap said. "Lazy shits who will never be *sooperheroes.*"

"Why does Enzo bother you so much?"

"The Unmighty Thor? She's a pain, that's why."

"She's nine."

"What's your point? I was nine once, too."

Zap's shoulders were tight with tension and he looked down at Joseph from his height. Joseph had once been tall. Sometimes he looked at Big, at the back of Big, and measured himself against this man who would not look at him. I would be taller than Big now, Joseph thought, if I were the way I used to be.

Joseph put his hands on the tires and pushed.

"Godspeed to the beekeeper," Zap said, and saluted.

Joseph shoved, and shoved again, and got into the rhythm. Now the PIG car was far behind, two blocks and more. Shove. Shove. Shove. Down Hennepin he rolled, past the apartment buildings with the striped awnings and the fake flowers in the window boxes, past Magers & Quinn Booksellers, past Calhoun Square, past the Uptown Theater and up the slight incline past the Y with the huge windows. People running invisible mountains. Biking invisible roads. Shove.

Joseph rolled past a small redbrick school with windows that opened directly onto the sidewalk. Some of the children in this school had aides who held their hands, or stood beside them as they pushed their walkers.

Cha appeared in the window, Cha who was one of eight people in the world. He gazed at Joseph with his calm eyes, and raised his hand.

Greetings, fellow wayfarer. I am the captain. Welcome to my ship.

Farther back in the room stood the teacher. Her hand was on the light switch. Joseph wanted to see the magic moment when she flipped the switch. The magic moment had not yet happened because the children were milling. That's what children did. They milled. They swarmed. They clustered around tables, all of them standing except for the ones who were strapped into wheelchairs. They bent over projects involving milk cartons and pipe cleaners, and bottles of white glue and pots of paint. Joseph sat outside the window and watched.

The teacher's hand still hovered over the light switch. What time was it? Almost time.

Flick.

The milling children looked up. Put the lids back on your paint jars, children. Carry your brushes to the sink and wash them. Do not burn yourselves under the hot running water. Everything has a place, and everything in its place.

Cha stood leaning against the window and gazed at Joseph, and Joseph gazed back at him.

"Greetings, Captain," Joseph said.

Cha said nothing. Speech was not of his world. He raised his chin and Joseph inclined his head in response. Joseph was first mate of the ship, greeting the captain's distinguished guests as they walked up the gangplank. None of them knew that the captain was a superhero in disguise.

Joseph would make sure that a porthole was open for Cha, so that in the dark night hours the superhero could escape, could swoop and circle the darkness of the storm-tossed sea. Fear not, Joseph said silently to Cha, who was now waiting by the window with his hand raised, your secret is safe with me.

"Excuse me?"

It was the light switch–flipping teacher. She stood next to Cha with her arms crossed.

"May I help you?"

Joseph sat in his chair and pictured himself through her eyes: a sixteen-year-old boy with hair past his shoulders, a rubber band holding it back. Did she wonder why he was in a wheelchair? She might be thinking of him as a bad kid, a kid who had been at a party in the Phillips neighborhood or a party in north Minneapolis, a party with no adult supervision, a party turned ugly, drugs, a turf war. Gunshots, and a boy's severed spinal cord. Where were this boy's parents? Who was looking out for him?

"Are you looking for someone?" the teacher said.

Cha stood at the window with his calm eyes. The teacher folded her arms and waited.

"I just moved here," Joseph said. "I've only been here a month."

The teacher frowned. And? So what?

Joseph could explain that his home was far away, that he and his father had driven long days to come to this land of no mountains and no oceans, and that his father was sleeping now, and that if only he, Joseph, could stand up, he would be taller than his father, and that he used to run, and that his mother was in a hospital, back on the island of bees. Was he looking for someone? He was looking for his mother, but she was not here. Everywhere Joseph went, his mother went with him, but she was nowhere that he was, not even on the playground, and she had loved playgrounds. He had gone to the playground with his mother every day. They had left their Scrabble game unfinished and walked to the Addison Miller playground, where over time the slide became a mountain, and the wading pool a small ocean that could sometimes be crossed and sometimes not.

But this teacher would not hear what he was saying. This teacher would gaze at Joseph's mother climbing her mountain, crossing her ocean, and this teacher would narrow her eyes. This teacher was on full alert for those who might harm her charges. She would defend them to the death.

"Can I help you with something, then?"

She would wait no longer. She was an army of one, this teacher, an unanonymous superhero unafraid to stand out in a crowd.

"I'm on my way," Joseph said.

The teacher inclined her head and did not blink. Be on your way, then—that was what that look meant. Joseph set his hands on the tires and shoved.

Six

"Go away," Enzo said to Zap. "You're interrupting the Game of the Century."

"I'm not interrupting. I'm merely observing."

Enzo flicked her fingers in his direction. "Shoo."

Zap retreated to the next table, where he draped himself on a backward-facing chair. Enzo and Joseph were playing the Scrabble Game of the Century. They would play to the death, Enzo said. When the rapture came, she and Joseph would not ascend on the stream of light, but instead remain on earth in order to finish their game; they were in it for keeps. That was Enzo's decree.

She had placed the salt and pepper shakers and the napkin holder between her tray of tiles and the bee dish, a makeshift shield between her and her bee enemies. A wasp muddled through the puddle of lemonade, laden with liquid sugar.

"Get lost," Enzo said to the wasp. "Fly away to Zap world. Nobody here wants you."

"No bee in his right mind would be caught dead in Enzo world," Zap said. "Enzo world is a cold and unwelcoming place."

Enzo ignored him and frowned at her tiles. She picked up three and set them into the three spaces descending from the *S* of **C A V E S.**

"*Star.* That's six."

"If you put it up there on the triple word, you could get eighteen," Joseph said.

"Maybe I don't want eighteen. Ever think of that?"

"Maybe he's trying to help you," Zap said. "Ever think of that?"

"He thinks he's so good at Scrabble."

"That's because he *is* good at Scrabble. And you've spelled two words wrong and used a proper name for a third. You are losing the Game of the Century. Yet when the beekeeper tries to help you, you reject his help."

"Who would want his help?" Enzo said. "He's the worst superhero in the world. He can't even fix his own legs."

"Maybe you should broaden your definition of *superhero*," Zap said. "Maybe you should quit being so mean."

Enzo bent over the Scrabble board. "I know you are, but what am I?" came muttering from her bent head, and then she shoved herself away from the table and was out the door. Zap reached for the score pad, which was covered with Enzo's clickster scrawls.

Mighty Thor: 38. Sooperheroe: 271.

"Not bad there, sooperheroe," Zap said.

"A superhero would fix his legs," Joseph said. "My legs are not fixed. If A equals B and B equals C, then A equals C. Therefore, I am not a superhero."

"I know more than you think I know."

Zap looked at Joseph, but Joseph turned away. The letters that made up the words on the board sat stolidly in their square boxes. They were kept apart from one another, unable to communicate. They could not see that they were part of a greater whole, a whole that was a word, a word joined to other words. What were the words of this, the Game of the Century? *Star. Riddle. Oxen. Wax. Jerk. Dummy. Mad.* The Game of the Century was nothing more than word salad, letters tossed together, no greater meaning to be found.

"Big was here earlier," Zap said.

"Yeah?"

"Yeah. Him and his little buddy, fresh from their morning libations."

Zap banged shut the cash register drawer and took up the broom.

"Was he always like this?"

"No. Back home he was different. He used to be a mixer, back at the bakery in Utica."

"And what else?"

"He worked at night. He came home when I was getting up."

"And?"

"He used to bring us stuff to eat from the bakery."

Zap drew the broom in long, slow strokes across the black-and-white tiles, sweeping up crumbs and dust and bits of paper.

"He does all that stuff now, doesn't he?" he said. "And he didn't just start drinking once he hit the flatlands, did he?"

"No."

"So what's the difference?"

There was a difference. But the difference was not easy to point to, and the difference came to Joseph in images and sound, not words. The sound and the look of the way it used to be: Big's voice in the kitchen, talking with Joseph's mother. The smell of the bread he brought with him in the brown paper bag with the end open so that the bread could cool and not get mushy and soft. A tiny loaf that he made for Joseph only, baked in a miniature white glass baking pan.

"He used to bake me this little loaf of bread," Joseph said.

"He still does bring you bread," Zap said. "I see him wandering around with it every morning."

When Joseph woke, a loaf that Big had taken from the early baking was waiting for him in a brown paper bag. Big would come home, set it on the kitchen table alongside the butter dish and knife, then head out to Liquor Lyle's.

The wings of the lemonade-laden wasp lifted and lowered. The lemonade was nearly dry now, coating the wasp with invisible sugar.

"Your father doesn't look at you," Zap said. "You ever notice that?"

Now the wasp hauled itself up into the air and zigged its way to the screen window, bumbling from corner to corner. No. No way out. Now the wasp zagged its way to the open double doors. Maybe when it returned to the papery nest, the other wasps would cluster around it, craving its sugar. Maybe they would swarm around the sweet wasp. Maybe they would devour it.

"So," Zap said. "You still in touch with your pretty girl-friend who was at the hospital?"

Joseph rolled to the big sink. The blue scrub bucket was wedged behind it, next to a stack of old sponges.

"The windows need washing," Joseph said.

"Not going to answer me?"

"They're dusty. You can barely see out of them."

Joseph turned on the hot water and placed the blue bucket under its spill. Water tumbled from the tap, frothing and foaming. Now steam began to rise from the bucket. The noise of the tumbling water nearly drowned out Zap's voice. Joseph squirted vinegar into the bucket and inhaled the sharp scent. He turned off the tap, hoisted the bucket into his lap, and positioned it securely on his legs. A backward shove on the left tire, a frontward shove on both, and he was sailing to-ward the dustiest of the front windows.

"It appears," Zap said into his baguette, "that our hero is no longer in touch with his pretty girlfriend who was at the hospital."

Joseph crumpled sheets of an old *City Pages*. Smudgy black-and-white photos of girls with big hair and parted shiny lips gazed up at him: *Call now. Hottest Twin Cities babes standing by. Live chat. All credit cards accepted. Must be eighteen.* The old sponges floated at the top of the scrub bucket. He raised one to the dusty window and the vinegar water flowed down the window, down his wrists, onto his legs. His jeans turned dark and a faint vinegary smell rose into the humid air. He turned the sponge to the rough side and scrubbed at the window, as high as he could reach. Then he turned it over and rubbed with the soft, spongy side.

"The hero is not forthcoming," Zap said. "The hero holds his cards close to his chest."

The crumpled *City Pages* squeaked on the drying glass. Joseph rubbed first in circles, then in long up and down strokes. The first window was finished and Joseph rolled himself to the double doors. Over the hump. The first day he had gone out on his own in his chair, he had gotten stuck on just such a hump. It was impossible to get over, that inch-high slope on the sidewalk in Utica. Back and forth he had rolled, trying to get up enough speed to make it over.

Back then, he had almost tipped out of the chair and landed on the pavement. Back then, he had almost vomited with the fear of falling. Back then, he could not have foreseen that buckets would one day sit steady in his unfeeling lap, that he would learn how to navigate the heaves and buckles, that from his chair he would look up and gauge how tall he would be, were he standing, in relation to those he now tilted his head up to see.

Outside, Joseph scrubbed the window and wiped it dry. Inside, Zap was talking into his baguette, something about the hero and his fall. Joseph rolled back into the bakery.

From the cash register, the window that Joseph had cleaned looked as if it ended halfway down the frame. The clean half vanished into the summer air, sun flowing through the pane as if it were air itself. But the top half was mottled with dust and grime.

"Another question? Yes, ma'am, you're on the air."

Joseph rolled back to the window. He took the stick wedged next to him in the chair, the stick he used to punch the handicap button at Jim's Gy . . . m, and tried to spike it through one of the wet sponges. If he could spike the sponge onto the stick, he could raise the stick above his own level and clean the window, clean the dirty, untouchable window.

"You have a lovely voice, ma'am. Has anyone ever told you that you sound as if you'd be a pretty goddamn hospital girlfriend yourself?"

Vinegar water ran down Joseph's arm, but the sponge would not spike. Joseph tried again, aiming the stick at the sponge and driving it forth. The window was disgusting. The window was repulsive. The window made him sick and he was on the verge of smashing it because of its ugliness, its filth, its un-reachability.

"Excuse me, listeners, but there seems to be a disturbance in the force."

The stick snapped and the sponge tore, a gash that ripped it in half.

"Jesus," Zap said. He tossed down his baguette and threaded his way through the tables to Joseph. "Don't get all crazy on me now."

"I can't reach," Joseph said.

He did not look up at Zap. He jabbed upward with the stick, toward the dirty half of the window.

"So you can't reach," Zap said. "Big fucking deal."

Joseph was soaked. The bucket of vinegar water had spilled from his lap and rolled under a window two tables away. The gashed sponge lay on the table before him, oozing water.

"Sponge killer," Zap said. "That little scene scared away our callers, you know. They fled the phone lines and the show wasn't even half-taped."

Zap plucked up one of the sponges from the floor and reached to the top of the window. In a few easy motions, he had cleaned the top half. Then he was outside, and the outside half was finished, and then he was back inside, and the entire window had taken him no more than a minute. Joseph sat in his chair, his jeans soaked through, faint vinegary waves of scent rising.

"Hey, hey, hey," Zap was saying now to Joseph. "It's all right, man. Just water. No big deal."

Joseph pushed himself out the bakery doors and wheeled around to lock up for the night. Zap had already left. Inside, all the lights were turned off, and the fans were stilled, and the chairs turned upside down on top of the scrubbed tables. The pale yellow walls were lit by the evening sun, and the blackboard had been washed clean of the day's soups. The bakery was silent, gathering itself for the dark night hours to come. Half a night from now, a key would turn in the door off the back alley and a tall man would enter. The tall man would walk to the ovens, which would already be heating; the mixer would have turned them on. Big would check the temperatures and adjust them. Then he would begin the baking.

Would the radio on the flour-dusty shelf above the wash sink be turned on? Music or a talk show? Would the mixer and Big say anything to each other?

Joseph would be sleeping when Big left. Big would be at Liquor Lyle's when Joseph left. Big would be sleeping when Joseph returned. He's a goddamn hero, Big might say to his friends at Liquor Lyle's; my kid's a goddamn hero. They would nod and agree. A toast to Joseph, the goddamn hero.

In Utica, Big had turned away from the window in the hospital room and come toward Joseph with his hands out.

"Joseph," he had said.

This was Big, returned to the foothills from the vast plains of the Midwest. This was Big, who had not come home from the bakery in Utica one morning, who sent money orders from Minneapolis. This was Big, who had told his mixer friend Nico to let Joseph and his mother know where he was. "He's going to bring you out there," Nico had said. "When he's got the money together." This was Big, who had told the landlord that they would need a ramp

"A ramp?"

Joseph stayed in the truck during the negotiations. The truck was not handicap-equipped and Big had to lift him in and out. Lawn mowing and snow shoveling and gutter cleaning and leaf raking and window cleaning = rent reduction + ramp.

"A wheelchair ramp, yeah. But I can build it."

Their voices had floated back to Joseph. The landlord tilted his head at his father, and then Big jutted his head backward in the direction of the truck, in the direction of Joseph. Joseph had flexed his arms and looked at his muscles jumping. They were new muscles. Chair muscles. "You'll see," John Schaefer had told him. "You'll be surprised how fast it happens. Just keep pushing."

"That your son in there?"

"Yes."

"What's the problem with him? If you don't mind my asking."

"His legs don't work."

"Accident? Hunting?"

"No."

The landlord waited. When people wanted more, they waited, and it took them a few seconds before they realized that they weren't going to get any more information. Then they either withdrew and got nasty or started talking faster. The landlord talked faster.

"A ramp, okay. A ramp. You said you could build it?"

Nod.

"Well, okay. We're all set, then."

We're going to need a ramp. And now we have a ramp. And look, here we have a boy who pushes himself up ramps and brakes himself down ramps. Here we have a boy whose arms hurt and burn. Here we have a boy with arms so muscled from pushing and pulling himself around the lake and up and down the pool that he could push himself up any ramp, but there are few ramps in the world, and many staired ascents.

Joseph pushed the keys to the bakery down deep in the pocket of his jeans. Tonight, after he swam, after he returned to the dark apartment, damp and smelling of chlorine, he would take the keys out of the jeans. He would place them on his bureau. In the morning, when he rose, he would reach up and feel for the keys and return them to his pocket for the day.

Joseph pushed off down the pavement. *If you had an electric wheelchair you could go faster than them.* Joseph was a para, not a quad. Joseph was a boy with a lower cervical vertebral fracture with accompanying spinal cord injury, and John Schaefer had told him to use a self-powered wheelchair. "That'll keep you strong," John Schaefer had said, "but can you handle it? Are you tough enough?" In the beginning, Joseph's hands had been raw and aching. In the beginning, an inch-high heave in the sidewalk could nearly topple him. In the beginning, the slope of a sidewalk cut at the end of a block had been a miniature Everest. And now Joseph's arms were like legs themselves. Now they carried him without complaint.

Seven

Zap snapped his fingers in Joseph's face, another of the small physical motions, like caramel tossing, at which he excelled.

"Come back, flyboy," Zap said. "Come back, come back, wherever you are. You wouldn't want to miss your girlfriend, would you?"

Mai floated through the open double doors of the bakery, jeweled sandals on her feet. A single wide band held them on, a band covered with embroidered vines of green, from which bloomed flowers of colored sequins and silver embroidery thread, flowers not of this world, flowers from some imaginary island.

"The Lovely One returneth," Zap said.

Joseph concentrated on the half-off platter, arranging

day-old muffins—blueberry, apple cinnamon, morning glory, and orange cranberry.

"My name is Mai."

"My name is Zap."

"Zap? What kind of name is Zap?"

"A perfect name for a superhero, of course."

Zap had threaded soda can pop-tops onto red yarn and woven the strands throughout his hair today. He clanked gently when he moved.

"Those sandals make you, what, three inches taller?"

She looked down. Joseph's head was bent over his muffin tray and he saw her face reflected twice in the display case window, once right side up and once upside down. She was her own twin. She wove her fingers through her river of black hair as if she were braiding, but no braids appeared.

"Hey, Mai," Zap said. "Maybe you too could be a super-hero. The Girl Who Always Wanted to Be Tall. And when your accident happens, you suddenly have the ability to stretch."

"Accident?"

"You have to have an accident to gain a superpower. It's part of the superhero contract."

"What if I don't want to have an accident?"

"Join the crowd, then."

Mai looked down and behind the counter at Joseph. Then she was standing in front of Joseph's display case, where the tray of muffins sat silent in the sun.

"Hi," Mai said.

Her toenails in the jeweled and sequined sandals, through the double glass of the display case, glowed iridescent blue.

"Hi."

"I saw you last week," she said. "Outside the school on Hennepin. You were talking to my brother."

"The Captain?"

"How did you know that's what I call him?"

"Flying Joseph knows all," Zap said. "He has come to save us from ourselves."

"Do you need saving?" Mai said to Zap.

"The world needs saving. Don't you ever read the head-lines? TEENS PERISH IN PROM-NIGHT DRUNK-DRIVING ACCI-DENT. CHILD ATTACKED AND KILLED BY SWARM OF ANGRY BEES. BOY FALLS OFF PRECIPICE, PARALYZED FOR LIFE."

"BAKERY GUY NEVER SHUTS UP, CUSTOMERS KILL SELVES FOR RELIEF," Mai said.

"Are you referring to moi?" Zap said. "Because if you are, I riseth not to thy bait."

A woman at the counter cleared her throat. She was short and she wore a green felt hat with a feather in it.

"Excuse me?" the woman said.

She had a voice that sounded like a little girl's, high and thin and full of air. Joseph could tell that Zap was trying his best not to laugh. His shoulders were held back and his eyes were wide and polite.

"Welcome to the temple of sweetness, madame. And how may I help you?"

"I don't think you kids are being funny."

"Funny?"

"I overheard you talking," the woman said. She held two loaves of honey whole-wheat bread and a pound of Hope Creamery butter. "You shouldn't joke about things like that."

"Who says we're joking?" Zap said.

"Those things really happen, you know," the woman said. "There's nothing to laugh at in a prom-night accident or a child killed by a swarm of angry bees. You shouldn't make fun of other people's tragedies."

The woman nodded significantly at the far window, where Kilt Man stood stiff and straight, his lips moving rapidly.

"People suffer," the woman said.

"That's the whole point," Zap said. "Why do you think superheroes were invented?"

"Still," the woman said. Her green felt hat with the feather bobbed as she rocked from one foot to the other. "Still," she said again.

She turned to Joseph. "How do you feel about this?"

Silence.

"Jesus," Zap said. "Lay off the guy, would you?"

"I'm just saying."

"Yeah. Well, just *say* somewhere else, Robin Hood."

The woman stared at Zap and then reached up and touched her green-feathered hat.

"Oh. I didn't know that was still on."

"Well," Zap said, "it is."

The woman put a five-dollar bill on the counter, next to the Auntie Apple's caramels bowl.

"Just think about what I'm saying," she said. "That's all I ask."

She headed down the sidewalk. Joseph watched her. She tried to walk slowly and with dignity, but a few steps out of the bakery, she took off the green hat and pushed it down into the paper bag that held the loaves of honey whole-wheat bread and the block of Hope Creamery butter in its green-and-white wax paper wrapping.

"Adults," Zap said. "I hate them."

Zap picked up the five and clanged open the cash register and shoved it into the fives slot. A soda pop-top swung near his eye and he reached up and ripped it out of his hair, a clump of wheat-colored frizz along with it. The Figurehead emerged from his back office and squinted into the bakery. He crooked his finger at Zap and Zap sighed and headed over to the doorway. The Figurehead's hands moved as he talked, and Zap nodded and kept nodding.

"I keep hearing this story," Mai said, "this story about you being the only boy in the world to fall off a mountain and fly without wings through the sun and the clouds into the deep blue sea."

"That's Enzo's version."

"What's the real version?"

"I fell."

Mai's jeweled sandals sparkled in the sun. She didn't shift from foot to foot, the way most people would.

"For real? How did it happen?"

What happened, for real, had happened in an instant. Months and months had gone by without Joseph falling, months during which Joseph was slow and patient and ever vigilant, and when he did fall, he fell in a flash. It still stunned him, how fast it had happened.

Joseph is hurt? What happened to him?

Is there any way you could come down here? He's hurt pretty bad. He keeps calling your name.

What happened to him?

He was at the playground. It was pretty bad. He's hurt.

But what happened?

We don't know. The kid's not saying a word. Except for your name.

Was that how Anna Micciolini had come to be at the hospital? Joseph would never know. He didn't know who had called her, or how she had gotten there. Maybe she'd walked. Maybe her mother or her father had driven her. Maybe she'd taken the bus. Joseph didn't think Anna had a car. Maybe she did now, back in Utica, the city he had grown up in, the home he hadn't seen since Big had come with his bent-over back and his outstretched hands and moved him here, to the land of Zap and the Mighty Thor.

"Keep pushing," John Schaefer had said. "Keep swimming. Work what you've got left. Swim and swim and swim." But what if you were tired? What if you had been pushing a long time, and your arms were quivering with exhaustion?

"I'm sorry," Mai was saying. "I'm sorry, Joseph. I was being nosy."

The Figurehead had returned to his cave. Zap was juggling Auntie Apple's caramels, three at a time. Higher and higher he tossed them, darting from foot to foot, the muscles in his forearms twitching as he caught them, one after another after another. The soda pop-tops swayed and clinked as he moved.

"I told you to leave him alone," Zap said. "You sent him back to his island."

"What island?"

"The island of bees."

Joseph's mother sat on the sand. She was wearing her dark coat. Her head was bent over something in her lap. What was it? A bracelet. Joseph's mother was making a bracelet out of tiny beads. They sparkled in the sun. She did not look up. She could not hear her son calling her.

The blue of the pool lay before Joseph, flat and mirrorlike. Joseph eased up to the edge of his side of the pool and braked. Braced his arms on the side and lowered himself. The old guy nodded at Joseph's legs, which were dangling underwater, and raised his eyebrows inquiringly.

"I thought you decided it was muscular dystrophy," Joseph said, loud enough to sail across the pool and right into the old guy's old-guy ears. Loud enough to be heard. Chlorine and sweat and airlessness and the chalky blue of the water all seemed to tighten up at the sound of the beekeeper's voice. The old guy in his yellow bathing cap stopped splashing his tiny handfuls of water on his legs.

"You talk?"

"I talk."

The old guy nodded. Just as he had thought; the kid could talk. He bent and splashed each leg in turn.

"You talk, but you say nothing."

The old guy's tone was conversational.

Arms out. And in. Sixteen laps—Joseph's age—and he stopped to rest. That was his routine. Joseph dangled in the pool, arms supporting his body, his body that was so light in the water, his body that was normal when it was in the water.

"What happened?" the old guy said.

"I flew."

"You flew. From where?"

The old guy's tone was measuring, inquisitive. He was turning the answer over in his mind. Flip. Flip. Flip.

"The top of a mountain."

"Into what?"

"Through the clouds and the sun, and into the deep blue sea."

The old guy bent forward with cupped hands. *Splash.* He shook his yellow-capped head definitively.

"No," the old guy said.

The old guy slipped off the side of the pool, flipped onto his stomach, and started crawling through the water, yellow no-flower cap bobbing.

Now the deep blue sea appeared before Joseph as he spiraled down from the heavens like a plane bound for hell, his own Joseph face a ghostly ripple in the trembling surf. Joseph was falling into the blue water, and the sky around him broke into pieces and the pieces fell with him, tumbling down around his shoulders, his legs. The sun pierced through the broken sky and blinded him, and there were the sounds of sirens and the stretcher and, far off, a woman screaming.

Nearby, an old man was cupping his hands around his mouth and calling across the pool to Joseph, saying that he, Joseph, was a liar.

Joseph watched his legs float down through the blue water until they hung straight. Gravity. The earth's core was pulling to itself the legs he couldn't feel. Come, legs. And his legs obeyed.

The old guy had long since shuffled out the door when Joseph left Jim's Gy . . . m. Joseph was usually the last to leave the gym, the man at the front desk yawning as he opened and shut the drawers of the counter in a complicated nighttime closing ritual.

It was always dark when Joseph emerged, dark and heavy with humidity that felt as if it could be gathered from the air, so thick did it hang. The sidewalks between Jim's and the apartment were always bare, deserted. Streetlamp light gathered at regular intervals as far as Joseph could see, far down these blocks that ran straight north and south.

But not tonight.

Tonight, the sidewalk was blocked. Bikes had been thrown down and a wheel spun in the air, glinting in the light of a far streetlamp. The feral children were off their vehicles and hunched over a crying child. Their T-shirted backs glowed white.

Shove.

Joseph skimmed over the sidewalk and eased to a stop next to the bent, hushed backs of the feral children. The crying child lay on her back, one leg drawn up to her chest. The hushed backs turned when Joseph drew up, faces sad in the twilit air.

"Jilly fell off," one said.

"Danny got too close to her."

"It was an accident."

The feral children drew closer together, shielding the fallen girl. Off the blurring wheels and hunched knots of their bikes, they were small; they were small children with the skinny legs and big round eyes of small children. Jilly held her knee and wept.

"Let me see," Joseph said.

They parted. Joseph leaned forward and placed his hand on the child's knee. Blood seeped from a scrape and she sobbed.

"You skinned your knee."

He reached behind him, into his black backpack, and drew out his towel. He placed it on the child's scraped knee and pressed gently. The child moaned and clutched her leg tighter to herself.

"Can you bend it?"

She could bend it.

"Can you stand?"

She could stand.

"Come with me," Joseph said.

The feral children looked at one another, eyes moving in wordless communication. The tallest one nodded; he was their leader. Each picked up his bike and followed Joseph down the sidewalk, one hand on the seat and one hand on the handlebars.

"Let Jilly go first," the leader said, and Jilly, limping, went first.

"You're the bakery guy, aren't you?" she said.

The feral children leaned their bikes against the brick exterior of the bakery. In the darkness, they followed Joseph inside. The streetlamp glinted off the coffee carafes and the salt and pepper shakers. Upended chair legs reached silently for the ceiling, a small interior forest. Joseph opened the display case and gathered a pile of cookies in his two hands.

"Here you go," he said.

The feral children took a cookie each, small Frisbees held in their small hands. Jilly had stopped limping. She took a bite of her cookie: oatmeal raisin.

"You're the one who jumped off the mountain and flew through the sun and the clouds," she said. "You're the flying boy."

"Yup," the leader said, "that's him all right."

"Did it hurt?" Jilly said.

She ate her oatmeal cookie in small bites, nibbling around and around the diameter of the circle. The cookie was shrinking in on itself as she ate.

"Of course it hurt," the leader said. "He fell onto the rocks."

The feral children winced and shook their heads as one, as if they had talked this over before, as if, among themselves, they had imagined the mountain, and the rock-strewn surf, and the fall.

"I'm not a superhero," Joseph said. "In case you were wondering."

The feral children exchanged another look.

"We didn't say you were," the leader said. "We're not stupid."

"It's only the mean pointer girl who says you're a superhero," Jilly said.

She made an Enzo face. She stood in Enzo's stance, arms

rigid and hand extended, fingers clutched around an invisible clickster.

"She's lying, right?"

The children studied him, waiting for confirmation, but Joseph was through talking. Their eyes roved over his chair, searching for possible signs of superpower, but no questions were asked.

"Well," Jilly said. "Thank you for the cookies."

The feral children filed out before Joseph and watched him as he relocked the doors. They got on their bikes and rode off slowly down the block, turned the corner slowly, and were gone. In the darkness, all their bikes were one bike, and in the brief glow of the streetlight, all their slowly revolving legs were the legs of a large sea creature that had found itself on dry land.

Eight

"This sucks," Zap said.

He threw his pen at the wall above the sandwich counter. It was one of the bakery pens from the mug next to the cash register, a blue ballpoint with a large pink zinnia taped to it. He crumpled the piece of paper on which he had been trying to draw Batman for Batman, who had been asking for one, and arced it into the garbage can.

"It looks more like a hermit crab than Batman," Zap said. "I can't draw worth shit."

"That's true," Enzo whispered, and bat-eared Zap lasered his gaze at her.

Zap plucked three Auntie Apple's caramels from the bowl and flipped them from hand to hand, then tossed one high in the air and caught it, and another high in the air, and another.

His juggling was ever more complex. Joseph scrubbed the tables, rolling from one to another with his sponge and a small bucket of hot, soapy water wedged between his side and the side of the wheelchair. The sponge was blue and rectangular and fit the palm of his hand. Enzo moved from table to table with him, using her clickster to point out spots he had missed. *Click.* Scrub.

Today, she wore a green San Francisco T-shirt. A tiny pocket was appended to the left sleeve.

"Can that tiny pocket hold anything?" Zap said to Enzo. "Like a clickster, so that we could all get a goddamn break from your incessant pointing?"

"Shut up!"

"No shouting in church."

"This isn't church!"

"To some of us it is," Zap said. "To some of us this is the church of sweetness and light. We say no to sour. We say no to darkness."

"I'm not in church," Enzo said. "And I'm not talking to you. I'm talking to the beekeeper from the island of bees."

Zap held up his hands and spread his fingers: surrender. He returned to the cash register, where a man on his cell phone waited for his latte, one finger up in the air to indicate something. Now Zap was ringing up the latte. Now Zap, too, was holding up a single finger in imitation. The man on the cell phone did not notice.

The doors opened and a stream of customers poured in. The first wave of churchgoers was out, and the churchgoers needed their croissants and their fresh-squeezed orange juice. The First Universalists mostly wore jeans and flat sandals.

The Catholics and the Lutherans dressed up, and if their children were still young enough to be dressed by them, their children were dressed up, too.

Batman ran to Zap and Zap scooped him up. Dozens of multicolored paper clips were fastened to Zap's braids, and his jeweled reading glasses sparkled in the sun. Batman reached for a blue paper clip and Zap held him at arm's length.

"May I help you, Batman?"

"I want one. I want a blue one!"

"One what?"

"One of those."

"I'm sorry, Batman, but you have come to the wrong place. This is a bakery. No paper clips here."

Batman slithered from Zap's grasp and Zap held up his tray of tiny paper cups filled with broken cookies, chocolate chips poking up like small boulders.

"One for you," Zap said, "and one for you, and one for you."

Enzo watched from her table. She lined her clickster up parallel to the salt and pepper shakers. Her cloud of dark curls was organized into a semiponytail and tied with a familiar clump of faded red ribbon. The heavy man's watch was secured to her wrist with what looked like a strip of duct tape. Zap passed the last cookie cup to the last toddler and Enzo watched it go by.

"What is that I see on your head?" Zap said. "I believe it's my hair ornament."

"You believe wrong."

"And what is that on your wrist?"

Enzo twisted her arm so she could read the watch.

"My watch," she said. "Do you need to know the time? Because it's 11: 03."

Zap's fingers clenched down on the rim of his empty tray. Enzo's shoulders were rigid. Then Zap turned and disappeared into the darkness of the back room. A woman at the counter, holding a beaded purse, cleared her throat and said, "Excuse me?"

Joseph rolled behind the counter.

"I'd like a peanut butter chocolate-chunk cookie and a fresh lemonade, please."

The woman's voice was bland and businesslike. She was an adult and she had no patience with easily distracted teenagers, these teenagers who took no pride in their work. Joseph bagged up the cookie and gave her some quarters and dimes and pennies in return for her dollars and pointed her toward the table where the lemonades rested on ice in their lidded plastic cups.

Across the room, at her table, Enzo clutched her clickster. Her head was bent, so that the mess of tangled ribbon was visible across the bakery. She wrapped her arms around her knees. Now she was a ball of child, curved into a corner of her brown velvet chair. Sometimes, when Enzo was not in the bakery, customers moved the brown velvet chair, wanting it for their own, and then Enzo had to drag it back across the black-and-white tile floor to her table in the corner. It was a light chair that looked heavy, and Joseph had once watched a tableful of old ladies stare at the child when she picked it up by its two front legs and hauled it behind her like a toboggan.

Zap emerged from the back room. He had been back

there a long time. Had the Figurehead called him in to the tiny office? Had he been talking with Julio the soup maker? Maybe Zap had been sitting in a far corner with his head against the wall, avoiding Enzo with her man's watch and her clump of limp ribbon.

"Hey," Enzo said. "I'm talking to you."

She rose from her chair and walked to the counter, where Joseph sat by the cash register. Invisible armor rose around her and she was impenetrable. An army stood behind her shoulder, a tiny army with sharpened spears and painted faces. The Mighty Thor was a child of consequence. The Mighty Thor would show the enemy.

"Did you even hear me?"

She aimed her clickster at the window, where the feral children were flying by.

"I said I hate them."

Jilly's hair streamed behind her and she flashed a grin and a peace sign at Joseph and Enzo. Joseph looked for a bandage on her knee, but she went by too fast.

"Her especially," Enzo said.

She turned to Joseph and imitated Jilly's two fingers, her wide grin.

"Her name is Jilly," Joseph said.

"How do you know?"

"She told me."

"What do you mean she told you?"

Enzo was on full alert. Her clickster was held between

thumb and forefinger, her eyes narrowed and boring into Joseph's.

"She fell down the other night and hurt her knee and I gave her a cookie."

"What do you mean?" Enzo repeated, as if she were searching for something hidden.

"I gave them all a cookie."

Enzo's eyes narrowed; the feral children had penetrated the walled city without the investigator's knowledge.

"They think I'm a superhero," Joseph said. "I wonder where they came up with that."

"I have no idea," Enzo said. "Because if you were a super-hero you would fix your stupid legs."

Enzo closed her eyes and put her hands over her ears.

"Stupid, stupid, stupid," she chanted.

"Jilly's just a kid," Joseph said. "Like you."

"I'm not just a kid. I'm the Mighty Thor."

"You're a kid."

Enzo raised her face to the ceiling and shook her head wildly back and forth. An animal sound came from behind her clenched teeth. She jumped up and managed to get her stomach on top of the display case, and now she hung, her head not far from Joseph's own, and at the same level. Zap came backing out of the storage room with a giant box of paper cups in his arms.

"Get off," Zap said. "You're blocking the view for the other customers."

"There are no other customers."

It was true. Customers had worked their way by ones and

twos and threes to the head of the line, and over time, the line had disappeared. Tables had filled with postchurch murmuring and the faint clink of silverware on plates and the rustling of waxed bakery bags.

Enzo held herself in perfect balance, her stomach centered on the narrow display case's top, her legs drooping down over the glassed-over muffins.

"This is an investigation," she said. "And you are not cooperating."

Enzo's army held spears at the ready. They massed behind her shoulders, squinting at Joseph with choleric faces. Joseph looked at her and waited. She pointed her clickster at his face.

"What was it like to fly?" she said. "Was it like a dream? Were the clouds soft? Were they like pillows? Did it last a long time and could you turn over and just float? Did you fall into the ocean? Was the water warm? Did you open your eyes underwater? Were the fish neon, like the fish in the pet store?"

"I don't know, because I fell."

"You flew."

"I fell, into a pool filled with snow."

Enzo shook her head. That was not the answer she wanted. There was no pool filled with snow on her island. She would refuse this answer and keep on looking for the correct one. Enzo's clickster dangled from the end of her slack arm. Duct tape secured the heavy watch to her wrist. Her head hung over the back side of the display case; she was a jack-knifed child. She let her head rest against the case and lifted her clickster and pointed it at Zap, who raised his eyebrows.

"Oh my," Zap said. "Someone call the cops. Girl with gun."

Click. Enzo turned back to Joseph.

"I want to live on your island."

"You can't," Zap said. "No savages allowed."

Joseph had no strength today to feel the anger of Enzo and Zap, and yet he felt their anger; it coursed through him and he had no way of fending it off. It was Joseph's job to keep Enzo and Zap apart, to separate the warring factions, but he did not know why they were at war. And Zap's voice was not the voice of an angry bee anymore; his voice was sad. Enzo and Zap were angry and sad bees and Joseph in his wheelchair was the beekeeper and the beekeeper was weary. Joseph picked up the blue sponge and rolled out behind the counter and began to scrub the tables. A fat bumblebee lay belly-up in one of the little bowls of lemonade.

"I'm not a savage," Enzo was saying to Zap. "But you wouldn't know that. You don't even know me."

"You won't let me know you."

Zap turned away from Enzo and picked up one of the Sunday *Star Tribune*s, for sale next to the cash register, and flapped it.

"Take a look," Zap said. "Everything going down, down, down, and it just gets worse."

Joseph kept scrubbing. The tables were sticky in the Minneapolis humidity, and they would not be less sticky once he was finished scrubbing, but he kept on scrubbing.

"And where is the superhero?" Zap said. "That is my question: Where is the superhero?"

Enzo moved to her brown velvet chair at her table in the corner. She banged the lead end of her clickster rhythmically up and down on the tabletop. The lead broke off with the first bang and then it was just metal. She had started this banging three days ago and Zap had made a sign and taped it to the window above her table: NO BANGING OF WRITING IMPLE- MENTS ON TABLETOPS. THIS MEANS YOU, IDIOT CHILD.

"Stop," Zap said, and pointed to the sign.

"Who's idiot child?" Enzo said. "My name is the Mighty Thor."

Zap walked into the back room and shut the door behind him. *Bang. Bang.* The tabletop was covered with dozens of tiny holes.

"Enzo," Joseph said.

Bang.

"Enzo."

"My name is the Mighty Thor," Enzo said.

Bang.

"Is your mother in the hospital just a blah old mother?"

Joseph circled the scrubber side of the sponge on a stain that would not come out.

"Because I don't want her to be a blah old mother," Enzo said. "I want her to be a superhero mother."

"My mother likes playgrounds," Joseph said. "She likes swings. And slides."

He did not expect to hear himself say that. His words sounded young, and foolish, like a child's. They hung in the air. A woman in a dark coat stood in a green-walled kitchen and smiled. Enzo frowned.

"Why?"

"I don't know."

Wary children like Enzo did not understand why a grown-up would want to sit on a swing and not swing. Wary children circled Joseph's mother and muttered among themselves. Enzo's face was tired, and her eyes were tired, and she sat in her brown velvet chair at her table by the window.

"Well, that's stupid," she said.

And then Zap was back, standing by the cash register, and Zap's face too was tired, and Zap's eyes too were tired, and the stain that Joseph was working on would not disappear. Something brushed Joseph's shoulder and he turned. Cha stood by the side of his chair, no eagerness in his gaze and no weariness, either. Nothing he needed to tell Joseph. No words pushing and straining from beneath, desperate to emerge. Mai held Cha's hand.

"Come on, Cha," she said. "It's not polite to stare."

Joseph saw the faint lines of a mustache on Cha's upper lip. He remained silent. It was near closing time on a Sunday, and Zap turned away and was already sweeping and beginning to turn up the chairs.

"He saw you," Mai said. "And he had to come in."

"Hi," Joseph said.

Mai's eyes were sad. They were not the calm old eyes of Cha.

"What?" Joseph said to Mai. "What is it?"

Joseph looked up into Mai's sad eyes, and Enzo was quiet and watching. Mai stood in front of Joseph with her blue shirt and her narrow shoulders and her black jeans and her black hair parted down the middle. Joseph placed his palms on his tires.

The day he fell, Joseph's mother had hunched on the swing at the Addison Miller playground, a dark creature, an animal caught in a trap, wanting but unable to chew her way out. She had wanted to tell Joseph something, and she had looked up and gazed at him, drawing him near with her eyes.

If he had had enough time, he could have drawn it out of her. It had been a strange January day, old snow clumped and frozen into the sand. Ice crystals.

Mai gazed straight ahead. Cha stroked Joseph's shoulder once with an extended finger, and then again.

"What is it?" Joseph said again to Mai.

"I'm tired," she said. "That's all."

This was how it happened. This was how people became beekeepers. They felt their burdens to be unbearable; they heard words unspoken, they held their own words inside, and they veiled their hearts. Again, Cha stroked his shoulder.

"Joseph is from an island," Enzo said to Mai. "An island of bees in the middle of the ocean."

"Really?"

"With palm trees," Enzo said. "And coconuts. And a mountain. And a mother."

"Really?"

Mai was being patient with the Mighty Thor. Joseph saw that her life had been a lesson in patience. He imagined her waking in the morning and listening for her brother. He pictured her making him the rice he had seen Cha eat with a white plastic spoon from a white plastic container that had once held yogurt. White on white on white, like snow on a slide by a snow-filled pool at a winter playground.

" 'Really?' " Enzo mimicked. " 'Really?' "

Her eyes were flat and angry. She banged the clickster into the tabletop. Cha made a chopping motion with his arm.

"He wants to go to the playground," Mai said. "He wants to go to his ship."

Cha chopped again at the air, but she didn't move. "Listen, do you want to come?" she said to Joseph.

"Where? To the ship?"

"Yeah," Mai said. "Maybe you wouldn't want to do that, though. Anyway, you have to work. Dumb question."

"The little kids at the playground call your brother 'Monster,'" Enzo said suddenly. "When he's standing on the ship. You know the way he stands."

Enzo gripped her clickster and stood with her back straight, staring.

"Did you know that?" Enzo said, and she sang a tuneless tune whose only words were *monster, monster.* "That's what they call him."

"Enzo," Joseph said. "Stop it."

"Enzo? Who's Enzo? My name is the Mighty Thor. And anyway, they do call him that. If someone were calling your mother back on the island Monster, wouldn't you want to know?"

"I know what they call him," Mai said. She spoke directly to Enzo.

"Well," Enzo said. "Okay. Just so long as you know. Even though it seems like if you know what they call him, you might try to do something about it."

Cha made the chopping motion again and jerked his head to one side. And they were gone.

"Nice going," Zap said from the cash register.

Enzo ignored him.

"Does your little sister on the island know you have a girlfriend?" she said to Joseph.

"I don't have a little sister. Or a girlfriend."

"So you say."

Enzo gritted her teeth. The tired red ribbon still drooped in her hair, and the duct tape strapping the watch to her wrist was wrinkled and fraying. One corner of the duct tape had peeled up, and the skin of Enzo's wrist was red and angry-looking underneath. Joseph placed his hand over the tired blue sponge on the pockmarked table. He could feel how much effort it took Enzo to gather her anger, to roll it into a ball, to send that ball powering through the air to Zap. She did it every day, and every day it was harder for her.

"What is that around your neck?" Zap said.

Enzo's T-shirt had slipped down one shoulder, revealing a necklace made of dozens of strung-together colored paper clips. She shrugged the T-shirt back up over her shoulder and gathered up her anger again and aimed it at Zap.

"Where did you get those paper clips?" Zap said.

"I found them."

"You mean you stole them."

Zap shook his head, a quick dismissal, and disappeared again into the back room. Disappearing Zap. The bakery was quiet in the late afternoon, and hushed. Sometimes it happened that a hush descended over the bakery, over the neighborhood, over the city. Maybe the hush descended over the whole world. Something was happening everywhere at once, and no one understood what or why. All that was known was the hush.

Bang.

Bang.

Bang. The clickster had taken a job on an assembly line

and it had to keep up. The clickster could not fall behind with the banging or it might lose its job, and then how would it support its family? The clickster could not stop or everything would fall apart. *Bang. Bang.*

It had been many months now since that day at the playground when Joseph's mother had hunched in the swing. The bright blue of the pool had not been visible under the snow, and the sun had broken free of its clouds and turned the snow to diamonds. Joseph's mother had sat on the swing for a long time without swinging. The silent children of the playground had circled the swing set, afraid to come closer but wanting to come closer. It was their swing and this alien woman was not welcome. Joseph's mother had pulled her arms out of her sleeves and wrapped them around her body, inside her dark coat, which had long ago lost its extra buttons. The empty sleeves had flapped and the children had not liked the way that looked. Behind Joseph's mother, the foothills of the Adirondacks had loomed against the horizon.

Bang.

It had been almost two months since Joseph had moved here, to this land of wide roads and no mountains, this land of angry child and bees to appease with lemonade sacrifices. The beekeeper had been swimming for a long time, and the bright blue water was threatening to close over his head.

Nine

The old guy waited across the pool, his skinny legs dangling in the water. The yellow bathing cap was on askew, so that one ear was exposed and his head looked a little deformed. He raised his eyebrows and stared at Joseph. Even from across the width of the pool, Joseph could feel the stare.

"So what does your mother think about you swimming so late at night?" the old guy said.

"She doesn't," Joseph said. "She doesn't know I'm here. She's back home."

"And where might back home be?"

"Upstate New York."

Words, tumbling back and forth through the contained air of the pool room. The old guy existed only in the pool; he had no life outside Jim's Gy . . . m. Maybe he was a figment of

Joseph's imagination, receiver of words that Joseph did not intend to speak. The old guy rippled his hand through the water as if he were a child playing speedboat.

"That's a long way away. When does the boy get to see his mother?"

"He doesn't."

"What kind of mother lives in upstate New York while her kid's out here in the flatlands? What kind of mother doesn't even know her kid's swimming late at night when he should be home doing homework?"

"There is no homework in summer," Joseph said. "And your bathing cap is on weird."

"So?"

"So your ear is going to get wet."

"Do I give a flying crap if my ear gets wet?"

Joseph shoved himself off from the side of the pool and flipped onto his back. Chlorinated water washed over his eyes and the lights went blurry. Anna Micciolini's face came to him.

So you don't know him?

No.

Not even as a casual school friend?

I knew who he was is all.

Did he have any friends?

Not really. I don't think so. He was really quiet. He hardly ever said anything. He was always with this woman.

Who?

I don't know. This woman. His mother, maybe? She always wore a coat. A winter coat. I used to see them at the playground.

Arms out. And in. And out. And in. Joseph swam fast and

hard for half a mile and then he was tired and he hung his arms over the side of the pool and rested.

"You're not a bad swimmer," the old guy said. "Strong."

He stood on his side of the pool. Every once in awhile he lifted a leg and stood balanced on the other. Skinny old heron in a yellow bathing cap. Joseph pressed the water out of his eyes with his two thumbs.

"Been swimming all your life?"

"No."

"You got some arms there, Kid. Don't lose them."

The old guy gazed across the pool at Joseph. His yellow bathing cap was still askew.

"Kid. You think I'm an old fart?"

The old guy's belly sagged over his swimsuit. His chest was chicken bones. Joseph could count his chickeny ribs. His arms were stringy ropes hanging off bone, and his thighs dipped inward toward his femurs, doorknob knees pressed together.

"Check me out," the old guy said. "I'm Rocky's uncle. I'm the man who taught him all his moves. I'm the unknown Stallone."

The old guy raised his arms above his head and pumped his fists into the air as if he were Rocky, Rocky as he would be in the final *Rocky* picture, when Rocky was an old man and his opponents had all died in their sleep of old age. Above them, the fluorescent lights hummed. It was close to midnight and Joseph wanted to be in the water again. In the blue, with the fluorescence stilled to silence and the water sloshing into his eyes, so that everything was blurred, then sharp, then blurred, then sharp. He wanted to feel the long, ropy muscles in his arms pulling him to one end of the pool, his hands scraping on the cement and then pushing him off again to the other end. Back and forth. The cement prison. The cement prison with its locked and keyless doors. The old man was talking again.

"Where in upstate New York?"

"An island," Joseph said. "An island of superheroes."

"She should bust her way out then. Come see her kid."

The old guy pumped his fists into the air and started humming.

"That's not the *Rocky* theme song," Joseph said. "That's the theme from *Star Wars*."

"You quibble," the old guy said.

His arms were down around his sides now.

"I used to be young, you know. I can see by the look on your face that you find that hard to believe. You take it for granted, Kid, but you shouldn't."

"Shouldn't take what for granted?"

"Your looks. Your health. Your strength. All of it."

The Unknown Stallone and Joseph were standing on the edge of a cliff, looking down at the blue, blue sea. The old guy's yellow bathing cap was so far askew that half of it bulged off his head and made him look as if he had a giant brain tumor.

"Youth is wasted on the young," the old guy said.

Joseph's throat closed up. He could not swallow. He was looking up at Anna Micciolini from a hospital bed in Utica, New York, and he could not feel his legs. The back of a man, his father whom he hadn't seen in over a year, bent over, his arms propped full length on the windowsill. Joseph knew that this was the beginning of the next part of his new life. He looked at his legs, long and still under the white bedspread, and he did not feel young.

"So tell me what really happened to you," the old guy said.

"So tell me why you wear that stupid yellow bathing cap," Joseph said.

The old guy touched his yellow cap. He looked surprised, the way that the Robin Hood woman in the bakery had looked surprised.

"This?" he said. "It was my wife's. She used to swim with me."

Joseph shoved himself off the cliff and into the blue and it closed over his head. And he closed his eyes and pulled with his arms and the water rushed cool and blue over his body. Over his shoulders and arms and chest. Over the muscle and sinew and skin that he could feel. Over the rest of him.

In the morning, Cha stood at the red rudder of the resin ship's prow, his fingers resting lightly on the spokes, gazing out at the lake, which was churned and rough with wind. At what did he gaze? Joseph turned to face the lake.

A kayak the color of flame arrowed its way through the water with the wind at its back, its double paddle arcing up and down, flashing in the sun.

Small children ran and splashed in the shallow water of the 32nd Street beach.

A teenage lifeguard in a red bathing suit, sitting atop a tall white ladder, blew her whistle and made threatening motions with her arms.

Two men stood arguing under a huge oak tree at the far edge of the playground. One wore a black T-shirt that read I DON'T GIVE A RAT'S, with a picture of a donkey underneath. The other man kept massaging his forehead with thumb and finger as if he had a headache.

A little girl sat on the far end of Mai's bench and licked an ice-cream cone. Green. Mint. Sugar cone. Occasionally she sneaked a look at Mai, as if Mai would make her stop eating if she noticed, but Mai's eyes were closed.

Three aluminum canoes, rentals from the Tin Fish Café stand down at the end of the lake, were pointed in the direction of the narrow channel that led from Lake Calhoun to Lake of the Isles. Over and over paddles flashed, but the canoes seemed to make no progress, bobbing in the waves and struggling against the whitecaps.

A toddler, with a girl who looked to be his baby-sitter next to him, stood at water's edge throwing stones.

A girl with a small black poodle looked furtively around and then slipped the leash off her dog's collar, and the dog streaked into the water and back out. And in, and out. And shook itself, a frenzy of water droplets spraying on the toddler throwing stones, who started to cry, whose baby-sitter picked him up and stroked her hand up and down his back.

Did Cha see all this? Was it possible to know what another human being was seeing?

Three small children gathered at the base of the pirate's nest and stared at Cha, their fingers jabbing upward.

"Look at the little monster dude."

"Can he talk?"

"Little monster dude! Can you talk?"

Cha gazed out to sea, to the rough gray sea. His fingers were light on the red spokes of the red rudder.

"Hi."

Mai stood beside Joseph's chair, next to the trunk of a tall oak. The oak leaves tossed and danced, and the floor of grass underneath was downtrodden and tired by the early August heat.

"Hi," Joseph said.

"It's not easy for the Captain today, with this wind."

The wind picked up and whitecaps ruffled the surface of the water. The human parade around Lake Calhoun trudged past, heading into the wind. The three canoes had made infinitesimal progress in their journey toward the channel.

"Where are you really from?" Mai said.

"Upstate New York."

"Do you miss it?"

Joseph's eyes stung. He nodded, and she nodded, too.

"What do you miss most?"

"I miss my mother."

"There's something wrong with your mother, isn't there?"

"There's something wrong with a lot of people."

Mai studied him.

"Don't forget who you're talking to here," she said. "I'm the keeper of the Captain, remember."

With the wind at their backs, two more kayaks sped along the shore. The paddle of one flashed up and down, a steady rhythm, while the woman in the second held hers up horizontally, like a slender wooden sail. Across the water came her laughter.

"You took care of your mother," Mai said. "Didn't you?"

Joseph nodded.

"Is it only her that you miss? Or is it partly the habit of taking care of her?"

Joseph's mother sat on the shore of the island, her dark coat wrapped around her, staring at her boy, her boy, who was falling through the air in long loops and curls. The kayaks disappeared at the far end of the lake. A small boy in a striped shirt stood at the shore and leaped at each incoming wave that bubbled and frothed on his toes. The world of Joseph and his mother was a narrow world. When Joseph thought of Utica, that was how it appeared to him: a world of narrow hallways and narrow routines, ever tighter and more circumscribed.

"It was a tiny world," Joseph said.

He wanted to tell Mai about it, the abrupt corners of that tiny world and how hard it was to navigate, harder and harder, but still that tiny world had been his world, his and his mother's. Mai was looking at him with her head tilted.

"Did you know at the time that it was tiny?"

"It was just the way it was," Joseph said. "It took up all the space I had."

"I ask you because I wonder about that sometimes," Mai said. "I don't know what it would be like to be without the Captain. And I thought that you might know."

The Captain gazed steadily out to sea. The little children were massing at the bottom of the rope ladder. One of them set a tentative sneaker on the bottom rung, which sagged under the pressure of his foot.

"Little dude!"

"Our turn!"

"Come on, Captain," Mai said. "It's time for us to go anyway."

She held her hand up to the pirate's nest and sang his name. Then she held her hand to her lips—Eat? Drink?—and Cha was sliding down the spiral metal tube in back of the pirate's nest. They made their slow way down the pedestrian path to the Tin Fish. Joseph had seen Mai buying Cha an ice-cream cone there once. A kiddie size, with the cone turned upside down into a cup, just in case.

The little kids watched them go, and then they turned back to the pirate ship. They would reclaim it from the boy who would not look at them, would not speak to them, who was their size but not of them. Joseph could feel Cha's brain within himself, its mazes, its walls and doors. The two of them were beings without language, without the means to articulate what it meant to be a beekeeper, or a wayfaring captain on a tideless inland sea.

Ten

"Wait, don't tell me," Zap said to the man at the head of the line. "Let me guess. Peanut butter chocolate-chunk cookie, am I correct?"

"You are not," the man said. "No sugar for me. Sugar'll kill you. Give me a small decaf with room for milk."

Zap frowned. Joseph could tell that Zap believed that a small decaf with room for milk was not the right choice for the man, but Zap held the wrongness inside and did not let it out, did not tell the man how much better than bitter coffee the cookie would have been.

Small decaf.

Six chocolate croissants.

A loaf of Asiago cheese bread. Sliced? Yes please.

Zap stood at the cash register, juggling his caramels between customers. He was up to four and trying for five. Whenever he added the fifth caramel, they all fell to the black-and-white tile floor, where Zap swooped down upon them as if they were runaway pet mice and flung them back into their striped ceramic bowl.

Mai and Cha sat by the front window, far from the countertop, which Joseph was scrubbing down in preparation for closing. No Enzo to point and click at the spots he missed; the angry child had not appeared today. A *City Pages* was spread open before Mai, and her hair curtained her face. Cha flattened a white paper straw wrapper with his thumbnail, and then he flattened it again.

"Tell me something, Flying Joseph," Zap said, too low for anyone else to hear. He pointed at Joseph's lap. "Does it still work?"

John Schaefer had said there might be questions. "You don't have to talk about anything you don't want to talk about," John Schaefer had said. "The answer is yes, you can still do it, and yes, it might shrink a little, but whose business is that but yours?" That was what John Schaefer had said.

"Because, you know," Zap said.

He glanced in Mai's direction, on the other side of the room. She did not look up. A new line of customers, anxious before closing, formed and Zap was trapped. No time to juggle, no time to talk about girls with long dark hair who sat quietly at tables with their wrapper-smoothing brothers, no time to speculate on the sex life of the superhero.

Mai and Cha came up to the counter.

"Wait, don't tell me," Zap said to Mai. "Let me guess. A

half-off brownie for the madame and a new straw for her manservant."

"Are you always so weird?" Mai said.

Cha raised his chin in Joseph's direction—Greetings, fellow wayfarer—and then he let go of Mai's hand and came around behind the counter. Now he stood beside Joseph, his calm eyes following the back-and-forth movement of the scrubber. Now he poked Joseph's leg.

"I can't feel that," Joseph told him, and Cha poked again.

Zap held out the bowl of caramels to Cha.

"Congratulations," Zap said to Cha. "You have won the grand prize of an Auntie Apple's caramel. Please, take your pick."

Cha ignored Zap and poked Joseph's legs again. Zap handed the bowl of caramels to Joseph with a shrug that meant, Good luck.

Joseph watched Cha's rhythmic finger: poke, poke, poke. Above Joseph's head, Mai and Zap were talking again. Words bounced around in the air, rebounding off the walls and floor and reverberating against the pressed tin of the ceiling. Joseph closed his eyes. He could tell from the movement of his leg against the side of the wheelchair that Cha was still poking, but he felt nothing. Poke. Poke.

Then a sound like hail filled the air, *rat-a-tat*, and Joseph opened his eyes.

The Auntie Apple's caramels lay scattered on the floor around him. They had leaped out of their ceramic bowl and jumped into the air. The bowl lay in shards on the floor.

"Little dude, leave the beekeeper alone," Zap said, an edge in his voice.

Mai crouched next to the wheelchair, one arm around Cha's shoulder. Cha gazed at Zap with his calm eyes. And then Mai had his hand, and they were heading toward the door, and they were out the door, they were leaving again, Mai was leaving, Mai was gone, and Zap was behind them, turning the OPEN sign to CLOSED.

Silence. The soft sound of fingers skating over the tiled floor. Clink of pottery. Whisper of waxed paper. Zap was picking up the Auntie Apple's caramels. Fifty cents each, 3/$1.00. Now Zap was collecting the ceramic shards into a waxed bakery bag.

"Flying Joseph," Zap said. He sang the nickname softly, as if it were a nursery rhyme. "Flying Joseph, Flying Joseph."

Silence. The slanting sun streamed in through the big front windows and illuminated the thousands of dust motes hanging in the air, the air of this bakery in the early evening, air lit and animate. Zap crouched on the floor before Joseph, his long arms like spiders, plucking up the wrapped caramels and, one by one, dropping them into a new ceramic bowl, a different bowl, a cream-colored bowl with a single navy stripe running around the circumference.

"Where do you go when you go away like that?"

Zap tapped the side of his head with a caramel. He gazed up at Joseph, his big shoulders and long arms draped over his crouching thighs. Power. Zap's body was power. He could spring up right now from this crouch, should he want to. Where did Joseph go when he went away like that? To a playground in upstate New York. A playground in winter, pool empty of water and filled with snow. He stood beneath a slide where a woman in a dark coat crouched, silent and shaking.

Joseph shook his head. Zap nodded and said nothing more. He placed the new bowl of Auntie Apple's caramels on top of the display case, then frowned and moved it next to the cash register instead, where no matter how short you were, you could see the caramels, soft and bulging, silky and sweet in their wax-paper twists.

"Tell me again where you're really from?"

"Utica, New York."

"Utica, New York," Zap mused. "I like the island of the bees better."

Pound.

    Pound.

    Pound.

The CLOSED sign jumped and jittered. Enzo.

"Go away," Zap called. "We're closed."

"Let me in!"

"Closed!"

Joseph maneuvered through the tables and the forest of upside-down chair legs reaching for the ceiling and flipped the bolt. Enzo came in, scowling.

"You locked the door," she said to Joseph.

"It was eight."

"You should have known I was coming."

Enzo stood in front of Joseph, a contained mass of angry child.

"I'm sorry," Joseph said.

"You could have read my mind."

She clenched her fist around the clickster and glanced

from Joseph to Zap and back again. Zap strummed an air guitar and sang in his tuneless way, thumbing invisible strings as
his left hand played a series of complicated invisible chords.
He was a folksinger in a small club, singing to a small, de-
voted crowd who had been waiting months for the chance to
hear their hero sing. He sang of the legendary Flying Joseph,
and of the twist of fate that had caused him to leave his ances-
tral dwelling on the island of bees and embark on the arduous
journey over grassland and plains, through the impenetrable
jungle, to end up here, in the flatlands of a new world, far
from the mountains and ocean of his home.

"Be quiet," Enzo said.

"I cannot be quiet. I am a troubador, sent to the outskirts
of the battle to entertain the troops."

"I said be quiet!"

She was in her Enzo world of clenched fists and rigid
muscles, eyes squinched shut and face pointed upward at the
pressed-tin ceiling she couldn't see. Her clickster pointed to
the ground. Enzo was sad. It shimmered off her in waves, this
sadness.

"The child does not like the troubador," Zap crooned.
"The child wishes him gone. The troubador's heart is
weighted with grief, and he takes his leave of the troops.
Farewell."

Zap walked backward down the counter, and backward
into the back room, still playing his air guitar. He would leave
by the back door, as he sometimes did, walking in the gloom
of the narrow alley between the brick building of the bakery
and the brick building of the fourplex next door.

Enzo leaned her head on the top of her knees and the

limp red ribbon dropped forward with her hair. It looked as if it had been washed along with her hair and had not come out the better for the shampooing.

"If I were a superhero, know what my superpower would be?" she said. "Hurting people."

"That would make you a supervillain then."

"Fine with me. I could be a hit kid."

"Who would you assassinate?"

"The people I hate."

"And who do you hate?"

"The people who don't love the people they're supposed to love! Duh!"

She turned to face the window and raised her shut-eyed face to the setting sun. Her body screamed, but her voice was silent. She was the subject of a scientist conducting a controlled experiment. The scientist held his laser pen over the little Enzo rat in the corner of the cage and trained the red beam on her pink eye.

"Like your mother," she said. "You love her, but she doesn't love you."

"She loves me."

"Not enough! If she loved you enough, she would be here with you."

"She can't. She's trapped on the island."

"Go rescue her, then," Enzo said. "Get out of that stinky pool you swim in and swim somewhere real for a change."

Joseph rolled a napkin around a fork and knife and spoon. He rolled it tight, so tight that a fork tine broke through the paper. He threw the napkin away and began again. Looser this time.

"And I would assassinate other people, too," Enzo said.

"Do you even know what *assassinate* means?" Joseph said.

"It means to hurt."

"It means to kill."

Enzo rocked back and forth. The merciless scientist kept the laser pen trained. The scientist was interested only in how far she could be pushed before she broke. He would push and push, until the child tumbled off the cliff, and then the scientist would make a note of how much pushing this particular child had been able to take.

"Whatever," Enzo said. "Like people who don't love their little sisters."

"Who doesn't love their little sisters?" Joseph said.

Enzo rocked. Beyond her, beyond her brown velvet chair, the sun was beginning to set.

"Is there no mother to love the little sister?"

Enzo shook her head.

"No father to love the little sister?"

Shake.

"No Mighty Thor to answer me?"

Shake. Her face was lit peach by the falling sun. The mad scientist had driven her to the end of the island, surrounded by impenetrable jungle. If palm trees and beaches existed on this island, Enzo didn't know where they were. She had no way to find them, no trails to follow that would lead her out of the undergrowth. The clickster sat on her table. Joseph reached out and took it. *My name is the Mighty Thor,* he wrote in the air. He drew an island in the air, a floating island surrounded by palm trees and waves. Time to call the angry child home, out of her jungle world, her world of no way out, her world of quivering clickster. Time for her to return to the hive, to calm herself in darkness. Joseph's fingers kneaded the thighs that he could not feel.

"What can I give you?" Joseph said. He was operating on instinct honed by experience, laying offerings before the feet of the bee child. *We say no to sour. We say no to darkness.* "A lemon square? A double-fudge brownie?"

The child's fists were clenched.

"An iced ginger cookie? A devil's food cupcake with cream cheese frosting? A piece of pecan pie? Banana cake?"

Joseph held up the bowl of caramels and shook it.

"A caramel? A raisin scone? A blueberry muffin?"

Joseph's voice was a murmuring creek. This had been his method with his mother. That day at the playground, given enough time, he could have called her home. Eventually, she would have heard his voice, and turned to him, and risen from the swing where she sat motionless, the center of the circle of silent children. If he kept going here, now, in the bakery, Enzo would yield. She would relax. Her eyes would go soft and her shoulders would loosen.

"No fists," Joseph said. "Uncurl those fingers."

Joseph spoke to Enzo as if her fingers were something not wholly within her control, something that didn't belong entirely to her but that she had the care of for a while. Joseph watched her fingers straighten.

"Enzo, look at me."

"Mighty Thor."

It came to Joseph that the bee child had been hurt and might not recover. He had felt this way with his mother, that day at the playground, when the murmur of his voice had seemed not to penetrate the impenetrable that surrounded her. But Enzo was a child. The right combination of words might still pluck the child up from her grinding anger, from the cliff she was heading down and down and down, her hands clutching for handholds.

"How about a round of Scrabble?" Joseph said. "How about a return to the Game of the Century?"

She trained her clickster on the window. Joseph saw that her heavy man's watch was missing.

"Pow," she whispered. "Pow."

"Where's your watch?"

Joseph rolled closer and picked up her left arm. The skin where the duct tape had held the watch on was irritated, an angry red.

"What happened to your duct tape?" he said.

"Nothing."

"Then where's the watch?"

She shook her head, then reached into the pocket of her shorts and dragged something out. She opened her fist and there was the watch, its plastic casing crazed, the hour hand broken entirely off. Enzo said nothing. Joseph maneuvered himself as close as he could to the brown velvet chair and put the brakes on. Her knees were drawn up to her chest and she wore one tie-dyed ankle sock and one grayish white one.

"Enzo? Are you crying?"

"Mighty Thor," she said. "Mightythormightythormighty-thor," and the name ran together, murmur without meaning.

Joseph reached out and put his arms around her, and she

leaned forward and curved herself over his knees and onto his lap, onto his thighs that couldn't feel her.

"You weigh nothing," Joseph said.

"I weigh sixty-two pounds," she said. "I'm the third-lightest in my class. Two people in my class weigh less than me. We did a bar graph."

"Then those two people weigh less than nothing."

"Does your little sister sit on your lap?" she said.

"I don't have a little sister."

"You do. You do have a little sister. She lives on the island. She uses a wheelchair, too, and she sleeps on the sand under a palm tree and she drinks coconut milk out of a coconut with a straw and she's never cold because it's always warm on the island."

The island had become its own Enzo world with its own Enzo rules, populated by trapped mothers and brotherless sisters who propelled their wheelchairs across white sand. All was possible on Enzo's dream island, with its palm trees and unbroken warmth and blue, blue Adirondack sea.

"If I was still on the island," Joseph said, "and if I had a sister, she wouldn't use a wheelchair. Her legs would work."

"How do you know?"

"Because," Joseph said, "she wouldn't have fallen."

"Why not?"

"Because I would have taken care of her."

Enzo pointed the clickster at Joseph. Her fingers did not move but the unheard click hung in the air, a weight without weight. Joseph could tell that she wanted to argue with him. But then she yawned. Joseph had never held a child on his lap before. Enzo sat on Joseph's lap, a feather, air, a curl of girl whose anger had turned to sadness. She had stopped crying and she breathed as if she might fall asleep, as if she might already be asleep. If need be, Joseph would keep murmuring of islands and sisters and palm trees. The right combination of words would be invisible ropes to carry Enzo away from the jungle, away from that spiral down, back to the world of lemon squares and brown velvet chairs.

Eleven

Zap stood at the bread counter, slicing bread for soup. A slanted slash, and then another, and then another. Zap was good with the bread knife. His arm moved just once, the bread crunched, and another slice fell to the wood. Zap's body was an athlete's body and he moved inside it without thinking. He scooped some soup into a bowl and arranged it and two slices of baguette on a plate and took it to Joseph.

"If I was a supervillain who hurt people, how would I hurt them?" Enzo said.

At first, it had been paralyzing rays that shot from her index finger. Then it had been a third eye that traveled about her body and could shoot paralyzing rays at will. Then a secret sonic vehicle that could shoot paralyzing rays from its headlights.

"I thought you'd already decided," Joseph said. "Some form of paralyzing rays."

Enzo tapped her clickster against her palm.

"I'm sick of paralyzing rays."

"So are we all," Zap said.

"Why are you sick of paralyzing rays?" Joseph said.

"Because they only work for a little while. Then their power wears off."

"I didn't know that."

"Well now you do!" Enzo said. "The evil guys are unparalyzed! You're back to zero."

"Make it permanent, then."

"Permanent?" Enzo held up her clickster and studied it as if it were new to her.

"Yeah. Permanent. Then the evil guys can never unparalyze themselves."

"Can I do that?"

"You're the supervillain, Enzo. You can do anything you want to do."

Enzo tilted her head and studied her clickster. Yes. Enzo was the supervillain. Enzo could do anything she wanted to do. She turned her attention to the plate that Zap had brought Joseph: the bowl of soup, the bread, a thick wedge of Hope Creamery butter cut from a pound block.

"What kind of soup is that?"

"Gazpacho."

"Eww. What kind of bread?"

"Sourdough."

"Eww. Who wants to eat sour bread?"

"Flying Joseph, apparently," Zap said.

"Who asked you?" Enzo said, and she screwed her face up and clenched her hands, and—Joseph put his hand over her tight fists.

"No," he said.

She stopped just as the first word was leaving her mouth. Joseph watched it swallow itself back down. The hive was alive with Zap-Enzo enmity and the beekeeper must step in. She opened her eyes and stared at him, and Joseph shook his head.

"No," he said again.

But the anger had risen within and needed a way out. Enzo swung her clickster through the air and pointed it at Zap, who was now juggling Auntie Apple's caramels behind the bakery counter, and extended the lead three clicks. She was a strange species of bee: a stalky, long-legged midwestern bakery bee, prone to anger and frustration.

"Enzo," Joseph said. "Do you want to play Scrabble?"

"Mighty Thor," Enzo said. "And it's too late. You missed your chance."

She stood before him, blocking his view of the Game of the Century.

"You had all those days to play, but you didn't play," she said.

"I was working."

"Working working working," she said in her mean grown-up voice. "Doing what? Protecting the world from bees?"

She reached behind her and crept her fingers spiderlike on the gouged wood of her table, feeling for the little bowl of lemonade. Tip.

"Guess what, you failed again," she said. "The bees are still everywhere."

The lemonade spread silently over the scarred surface.

"You're not a superhero," she said. "You can't do anything that a superhero would do."

"I know," Joseph said. "That's what I've been telling you."

"You can't keep the bees away, you can't make your legs better, and you can't rescue your stupid mother in her stupid hospital on her stupid island. You can't even win the Game of the Century, which by the way have you taken a look at lately?"

Joseph wheeled to the right and brushed past the arm that she extended like a crossing guard. The Game of the Century sat on the table, a perfect square of board within a perfect square of table. All the letters had been used. They crowded together in the middle of the board, each space taken. Rows of letters that made no sense together were placed against other rows of letters that made no sense in a thick and dense huddle, the unused spaces beyond like a moat separating the clot of words from the freedom and power of the double-word spaces, the triple-word spaces, the border-land at the edge of the field. Joseph looked at the angry mass of letters; it was a word search without words.

Enzo reached out one finger and began to trace the rows of letters.

"*Wylindrakull,*" she recited in a Kilt Man murmur. "*Slap-nubbery. Folpiterolved. Abudabinabukabi.*"

Joseph's hand reached out and gave the board a spin and the letters and words blurred. He gave it another spin and the spinning board rocked on its base.

"Stop it!" Enzo shouted. "You're wrecking the Game of the Century!"

Spin. The letters in their individual squares were threatened. A tidal wave was on the way and they shivered and jostled in their individual prisons on the island, unaware that there were others like them, that they were not alone. The tidal wave grew and grew, a gray wall of salt water rushing to swamp the tiny tiles on their unstable island, while the would-be superhero watched helplessly from his wheelchair.

"He's wrecking the Game of the Century!" Enzo cried.

She was talking to someone else, someone whose hand was descending from the air. A palm splatted in the middle of the wild board and the wild board came to a halt. Letters had been displaced. The nonsense words remained nonsense.

"Not everything is about you," Zap said. "Can you understand that?"

"You said he was a hero!"

"He is," Zap said.

"Then he should walk!"

"You can't always walk, no matter how much you want to, Enzo."

"Mighty Thor. And you can if you really want to. You can do anything if you want to bad enough."

Zap's hand still covered the mass of letters on the board. Underneath his palm, the letters were quiet and still. They were not alive. They were not biding their time, hoping that someone somewhere would make sense of them. The Game of the Century was a nonsense game played by fools.

Enzo gazed at Zap with narrowed eyes. Joseph could see her shift into victim-of-interrogation mode. She was sitting on a wooden chair in a black room. A spotlight shone into her eyes and her hands were tied behind her back. She had been without food, water, or sleep for days. Men she couldn't see were sitting behind an invisible desk and they might ask her any question they wanted, but she, Enzo, would never reveal her secrets. She pointed the clickster at Zap.

"Pow," she whispered.

Zap looked up and caught her mid-"Pow."

"What do you think you're doing?"

Silence.

"I said, What do you think you're doing?"

Zap's voice was quiet. An outsider to the bakery might think that he was making a simple inquiry, or trying to soothe an upset child. Suddenly, Enzo sat up straight.

"Paralyzing you!"

Now she was a proud supervillain who would gladly die for her bravery. She would reveal her secret power on her own terms, knowing the consequences, and die unashamed.

Her back was straight and her shoulders high. The battle was enjoined.

But Zap refused to fight. He plucked up the broom and headed out to sweep the sidewalk. The angry child sat at her table. *Click. Click. Click.* Joseph rested his hands on the tires of his chair and watched her. She turned to him and pointed her clickster.

"Do your legs hurt all the time?"

"Stop it."

"Do they?"

Joseph watched his fingers poking at his thighs. First his right, then his left. Back and forth. If thighs made music when you poked them, he could use his thighs as a piano and drums. He could travel about the country with his own act, the Wheelchair Boy and His Band. They could perform under striped tents.

"I don't feel anything," Joseph said.

That day at the playground, on the swing, Joseph had watched his mother poke her hands out under the hem of her dark coat and pick the skin at the sides of her fingers until she bled. Her empty sleeves had hung at her sides. The circling children had watched her pick her fingers, agitate them like small nervous animals. They had gasped when drops of blood fell into the dirty snow. Joseph had kept talking, the slow trickle of his voice a lure for his mother, who sat in the swing not swinging, but his mother had not turned to him.

"You do so feel them," Enzo said. "You're just lying."

Now Zap was outside the window behind Enzo's table, sweeping the sidewalk. Occasionally, he plastered himself against the windowpanes as if propelled by extreme force and mushed his face against the pane, eyes bugged and staring in Enzo's direction. Now he stood with his arms looped around the broom, twisting his face into grimaces aimed at Enzo, who didn't know he was there.

"Hello, hello, is anyone alive in there?" Enzo said.

Joseph kept his eyes on his bowl of gazpacho and willed himself not to look at Zap. What might Enzo do if she saw Zap making fun of her? She was an island child and she attended the laws of the island, which to an outsider might appear arbitrary, without reason or deliberation, but the supervillain knew otherwise.

"You lie and you lie and you lie," Enzo said.

A bumblebee circled above her in lazy swoops, droning past her face and then zooming up again.

"Assassinate that bee," Enzo said.

She shrank into her chair. Her eyes followed the progress of the bee, which was circling her head, its threadlike legs trailing below its furry body.

"It's not hurting you."

Enzo's eyes did not leave the bee. Outside, Zap jerked his head around and then staggered backward on the sidewalk, pretending to be riddled with bullets. An unknown assailant had found him, discovered him at the bakery, lain in wait until he emerged with his broom and began sweeping. Now Zap's hands were up in the air, but still the pretend bullets kept coming.

"I said assassinate it."

Enzo shrank herself even smaller than she actually was, crushed herself against the brown velvet of her chair. She followed the bee with her clickster as it circled ever closer to her head.

Outside, Zap tumbled gracefully, in slow motion, to the sidewalk. Now Zap was on his knees. Now his head was bowing forward. He was a dying boy and his eyes were closing for the last time.

Joseph knew that if Enzo turned and saw Zap on the sidewalk and thought that her sworn enemy was dead, something in her might break. He willed himself not to stare at Zap.

But he did stare at Zap.

Enzo saw his gaze. She turned her own gaze to the window, beyond which lay Zap's body splayed on the sidewalk. The clickster cartwheeled through the air and splatted against the window. Joseph's heart hammered in his throat, and his vision blurred from the adrenaline that Enzo's scream caused to burst within him.

"Enzo, no," he said. "No."

He wanted to tell her that it wasn't real, that it was a joke, that Zap was alive, but he could not; Enzo was beyond reach. The startled bee hovered above her and then zoomed off. Enzo's eyes were closed and she fought her way through a jungle, through tangles of leaves and branches. Her arms clawed toward the ceiling and she screamed like a child who had just witnessed the murder of someone she loved; she screamed for Zap.

Joseph rolled toward the door. He shoved himself over the hump and then he was through, and then he was out on the sidewalk.

He ran his tire right over Zap's hand, and Zap's dead eyes opened.

"Hey!" Zap said.

"Enzo thinks you're dead," Joseph said. He maneuvered himself again and ran over Zap's other hand.

"Lay off," Zap said. "It was a joke."

Next to Zap, the sidewalk heaved, jutting up one corner of the pavement. Joseph's chair ascended halfway up the heave and then fell back again. An invisible force field rose around the two warring factions. Joseph shoved himself backward with both hands on the tires, then forward, but the heave in the sidewalk was insurmountable. Joseph struggled for purchase on the edge of the cliff, warriors massed behind him and blue sea below.

"She thought you were dead," Joseph said. "She thought you were shot."

Zap crouched by Joseph's chair, rubbing his run-over hands. No blood. Their eyes were level, and Zap's eyes were dark.

"Were *you* shot?" Zap asked. "Is that the real reason you're in that chair?"

"She thought you were dead," Joseph said again. "Is that what you want to do to her?"

He could not seem to say what he wanted to say.

"She's just a little kid," Joseph said.

And then there was Enzo, her clickster held like a weapon. It had come to pass; something in her had changed. She stood before them, a child filled with poison. The bee-keeper had not done his job.

"I am not a little kid," the little kid said.

She turned to Zap. "And I don't care if you *are* dead."

She pointed her clickster at Zap.

"Die," she said.

She reached behind her and ripped the limp red ribbon from her hair and threw it at him. She tore the paper-clip necklace from her neck and threw it at him.

She pointed the clickster at Joseph.

"Walk."

Joseph sat in his chair. Enzo clicked the clickster again and kept on clicking. *Click Click. Click.*

"Get up. You're unparalyzed."

Joseph shook his head.

"Get up! You're unparalyzed now!"

And Joseph reached up and grabbed the clickster from Enzo's hand and drove it into his thigh. He took his hand away and the clickster stayed upright, a single drop of blood welling from the hole punched through his jeans.

"What did I tell you," he said. "No pain."

Enzo's fingers hovered and flickered above the clickster, spiders trying to trap the desperate fly, but the desperate fly was already dead. Sometimes things happened that you didn't think could possibly happen. You looked down from a great height, and the warriors behind you grew closer. They were on their way. They would not be deterred. You did not want to fall, but what choice did you have?

Joseph opened his eyes and shook his head at Enzo and Zap, sworn enemies crouching before him in his wheelchair. There were no words. No words gave voice to what he felt inside him, what he felt in his dead legs, legs that had no feeling.

"This is all we get," Joseph said. "Can't either of you see that?"

Enzo and Zap were still and silent and watching him. Joseph felt his own struggle for words as a physical presence among them. It was so hard in this world to say what you meant. He stood at the edge of the cliff, with the blue water far below. The warriors wanted what they wanted, and what they wanted was Joseph, broken and tumbling through the sky to the boulder that heaved itself from the heaving sea.

Twelve

"What happened here?"

A man's voice was talking. Under Joseph's cheek, the sidewalk was warm and grainy and rough. Joseph opened his eyes and shut them again. The sun was bright. He was in Minneapolis, this mountainless city, this city with its tiny inland sea.

"What happened?" the man's voice said again.

"He fell out of his chair," Enzo said.

"I can see that. How?"

"He just fell out." Enzo's voice was hoarse.

"You can't just fall out of a wheelchair. Were you kids bothering this boy? Fighting? Hurting him?"

"He was screaming."

"About what?"

"His legs."

The man came nearer and crouched next to Joseph. Joseph could feel his presence, and he heard him suck in his breath.

"Jesus," the man said. "Has he been stabbed? What the hell is going on here?"

Joseph opened his eyes. The man leaned over him, and then his hands were on Joseph's legs, and he pulled the clickster from Joseph's thigh. It came out easily, like a feather plucked from air. A drop of blood welled, became a tiny trickle, ceased.

"And his mother," Enzo said. "He was screaming about his mother."

The man raised his head and looked around. "Where is she?"

"She's trapped on an island."

"What?"

"He fell off a mountain trying to rescue her. That's how his legs got hurt."

The man squinted and shook his head in disgust. Island? Mountain? The kid was crazy. The kid was no help. The kid was lying to him.

"Is there an adult in this bakery who knows this boy?" he said. "Someone who can help him?"

"Who the hell are you?" Zap said. "You think you can just butt in here and take over?"

Joseph could feel Zap's breath on his cheek, and Zap's braids brushed his neck in their stiff way, like a pawing dog.

"He's injured," the man said.

"Of course he's injured," Zap said. "Leave us the fuck alone."

Joseph saw his mother sitting on a swing before him, her face obscured by the streaming sun. Joseph's mother was a blurry outline, the sun making a halo of dust and light around the dark bulk of her body in its dark coat. Her sleeves hung empty. She knelt down so that her head was on a level just above Joseph's and her face came into sudden and sharp focus. The beekeeper and his mother were displaced in time and landscape, far from the mountains of upstate New York, far from their home. Joseph's mother shook her head, and her eyes were filled with sadness.

"Mom," Joseph said.

"Where is this boy's mother?" the man said.

"Not here," Zap said.

"What about his father, then?"

"Sleeping."

The man nodded abruptly. A mother who'd disappeared, a father who didn't care.

"Here she is, Joseph."

That's what they had said, the last time Joseph had seen Anna Micciolini. Joseph couldn't see the someone in the room who was saying "Here she is." But he had seen that Anna was there. Why was Anna there?

"You were calling for her. Remember?"

Joseph had been calling for Anna Micciolini?

"Hi."

Anna had looked down at the floor and her lips had moved and she had said hi. Twice. She was not wearing her white sweater and she was not wearing one of her pale T-shirts. She was wearing a jacket with a ski tag attached to the zipper.

"You ski?" Joseph had said.

"Once," she said. "At Gore Mountain."

"Only once?"

"I didn't like it."

Those were the words that Anna Micciolini had spoken to Joseph: *Hi. Once. At Gore Mountain. I didn't like it.* Anna Micciolini was still in Utica. Maybe she was wearing her white sweater at this very moment. She'd had that sweater for all three years that Joseph had gone to school with her. Not that he had known her. He had never spoken to her. But still, he had seen her here and there. Walking up Genesee Street. Once in the gift shop of the Munson-Williams-Proctor Museum of Art.

In the end, Anna Micciolini had stood by the hospital bed and looked down at the floor. How many times had Joseph called for her? Who had brought her to the hospital? What had they told her? Had they just looked up Micciolini in the White Pages and called?

"Someone needs to call this boy's father and wake him up," the man said.

His voice was impatient and angry. This was a man who was not used to being ignored by teenagers, or by anyone. This was a man who wore a suit and strode through carpeted rooms filled with cubicles. This man was disgusted by what he imagined about Joseph's father. This man could not see the outline of Joseph's father's body against the window, see the animal of Big hunched against the hospital wall, out of his element, unable to move.

Joseph kept his head on the sidewalk still so that his tears would not fall, so that he would not begin to cry. If he began to cry, he might not stop. Now Zap was lying down next to Joseph. They were side by side on the sidewalk in front of the bakery on Hennepin Avenue.

"Come on, flyboy," Zap said. "Your chair's set up. Hang on to me and I'm going to pull you up."

"No," the man said. "You can't move him. He might have broken his neck."

"He broke his neck a long time ago, you dipshit."

"He fell off a mountain," Enzo said to the man. "Remember?"

Zap turned his head away from the man. Zap wanted the man gone. He was ready to put all his strength into Joseph, pull him up, cradle him, set him back in the chair. His braids hovered over Joseph's head. Zap gripped Joseph under the armpits, ready to lift. Ready to carry Joseph back to the world of chair, and bakery, and pool. To the room with many windows that was the bakery, where people stood by those windows, their coffee and muffins forgotten, and stared out at a Minneapolis summer day where a boy with a broken neck lay quietly on the sidewalk.

Joseph looked up and behind the impatient standing man, to the sky spreading away, a horizontal curtain of featureless terrain. Where were the mountains? Where were the old brick buildings and falling-down frame houses of Utica? The men his father used to work with had gathered silently around the truck the day that Big drove Joseph away. "So long, Big," they had said. "So long, Joseph. You two take care now, out there in Minneapolis." Nico, Big's mixer friend, had come to the truck and gazed at him. No smile. Then he had tapped on the window until Joseph rolled it down.

"Kid. Anything I can do for you?"

Joseph had looked into his eyes, dark brown and liquid. Nico had half-crouched so that he was level with Joseph in the truck. Not easy for him; he was a big man. Men ran big in upstate New York.

"Anything?" Nico said.

"Yeah."

Nico's eyes brightened. He looked almost happy. He could do something for Joseph. "Say the word, it's done."

"Please check on her sometimes."

Nico had turned his head away and nodded. Then Big came out and they got in the truck and drove away.

The standing man knelt and pressed something into Joseph's hands.

"Call your father," he said. "I don't care if he's sleeping. Wake him up."

The soft leather of the cell phone holster was warm in Joseph's hand. Joseph punched in the numbers and watched them light up the tiny green screen. The phone felt small and powerful in Joseph's hand, and his hand began to shake. The air was hushed and too still. Everything in the world was holding its breath.

Joseph punched the little red phone symbol on the keypad and the numbers disappeared.

He was still lying on the sidewalk, Zap's arms under his shoulders. Words swirled around him: Zap and the man, hard and angry words jabbing at one another, and the shrill of Enzo like a bird darting, protecting its nest. No more. No more of them, with their talking and their jabbing and their "Where is this boy's mother?" and "Where is this boy's father?" and now the man was standing with his arms out, saying, "Who is the adult in charge here?" and now the man was saying, "Call your father, this minute, or I call the cops," and Joseph was punching in numbers at random.

"Mom?" he said.

Zap and Enzo stopped fighting and turned and stared at him. The man nodded in satisfaction and crossed his arms: There. Now they were getting somewhere. This boy's mother had been notified and would soon swoop in and take charge of the whole sorry mess.

"Mom," he said again while Zap and Enzo stared. Joseph nodded with the dead wall of the phone pressed against his ear. He kept nodding. His voice sounded like a child's voice, like a boy, a boy too young to know how to hide his feelings.

"Hey," Zap said, too softly for the man to hear. "Flyboy. Big's on his way. The Figurehead called him."

Joseph lifted his head. Zap's eyes were narrowed and anxious.

"I'm sorry, man," he said. "I tried to stop him."

Joseph lifted his head higher and looked at the Figurehead, who stood next to the man with crossed arms. They were chatting, relaxed. The boy's father was on his way.

"He's a drunk," the Figurehead was saying, "but a controlled drunk. One of those functional drunks, know what I mean? And he's a good-enough oven guy. I'll give him that."

The crossed-arms man frowned. A drunk was not his preferred father figure. But it was no longer his business. He flipped shut his phone, reholstered it to his belt loop, and recrossed his arms. He would just wait here until the functional drunk appeared. He would make sure that the situation was under control.

Joseph looked down the sidewalk.

"Jesus," the man said. "Don't tell me that's the father."

Big's body at the end of the block was outlined against the sun. Now Big was shifting, turning into a blur, pounding down the sidewalk toward him, toward Joseph. A howl came tearing from his throat. In one motion, Joseph wrapped his arms around Zap's neck, Zap lifted him up, and Joseph was back in the chair.

The cell phone man shook his head in disgust. He understood it all now. The entire situation was clear to him. But nothing was clear, and the cell phone man with his crossed arms understood nothing. Could he see Big's back, bent over the sink when he got home, his hands cupped to splash his face, rinse the flour away? Could he see the shade in his bedroom drawn down and duct-taped to the sill to keep the sun out? Could he see the loaf of ciabatta in its paper bag open at one end, set on the kitchen table and waiting for Joseph to wake up, roll out to the kitchen, spread butter on a slice, and eat? Everything was so much more complicated than the cell phone man knew.

Big flung himself on the Figurehead and pointed at Joseph and cried. Joseph held up his hands: All is well. The boy is back in his chair and there is no need to worry. The Figurehead was saying something about a little fall, but everything was fine, and the crossed-arms cell phone man was saying that falling apart was not going to help the situation any, and Big was still crying, and Big was saying that his kid was a fucking hero.

Joseph looked at the crossed-arms man and held out his hand for the clickster. He kept holding out his hand until, reflexively, the man dropped it into his palm. There was only a little blood at the very tip, and Joseph wiped it off and gave it to Enzo, whose fingers were trembling, and whose hand closed around it, and Enzo ran into the bakery and to her table by the window. Joseph and Zap left the men on the sidewalk behind them and followed.

Thirteen

The clickster ground itself into the table, zigging and zagging across the scrubbed and pockmarked top. Enzo bore down so hard that the top snapped off and flung itself across the table to the window, where it hit and then dropped to the floor. Enzo kept on grinding. A long rasping sound, the animate groan of dead wood, rose from the scarred surface.

"Enzo," Zap said.

He moved like liquid through the tables, weaving and slipping sideways. He plucked the stunted clickster from Enzo's hand and held it, a dangerous object, above the table. Enzo reared up from her chair like an enraged animal and flung herself at Zap, butted her head against him and flailed her fists. Zap caught and held her easily. She squirmed in his grasp but could not free herself. Tears of frustration jumped out of her eyes.

"You need to go home," Zap said.

"He lied to me!"

Enzo pointed with her imprisoned fist at Joseph.

"He's a liar! His legs do so hurt!"

Zap panted with the effort it took to keep Enzo confined, keep her from scratching his face and eyes, keep the angry child from struggling her way to the ground and then flinging herself through the door and down the sidewalk to wherever it was she went when she left them each day.

"You need to go home," Zap said again.

"Where's home?" Joseph said.

"The island!" Enzo said. "I want to go home to the island."

"Home is fourteen blocks from here," Zap said. "She lives on Blaisdell, near the Quang Restaurant."

He held the struggling child in his arms and tilted his head toward the east, in the direction of Blaisdell.

"She lives with her mother and her father in an apartment on the third floor of a six-unit building," Zap said. "To get here from there, she walks south on Blaisdell to 26th, then she takes a right, then she walks to the corner"—he motioned with his chin toward the end of the block, where the sun was going down—"and then she turns left at the end of the block," he said. "And then she's here. And then she comes in through those doors"—he motioned with his chin toward the double glass doors—"and then she comes straight to this table."

Enzo was wilting. Zap held her with both arms wrapped tightly around her.

"And then she sits here with her clickster. And she gouges. And she bangs. And she hurts."

Enzo shook her head back and forth.

"And it's going to stop," Zap said. "Right here, right now. Hear me?"

He spoke directly to Enzo, his voice a quiet brook, trickling into her ear.

"You are going to stop," he murmured. "Enough. No more. No more now."

Zap's voice was hushed and sad. His arms loosened, and Enzo was pushing herself up and out of the big brown velvet chair, leaving behind her table gouged and scarred, and slamming the doors shut, so that the windows shuddered in their frames. The brown velvet of Enzo's chair held the outline of her body the way velvet did, crushed and retaining the form of that which had crushed it.

Zap plucked two caramels from the bowl and arrowed them toward the window—*bang*—they were birds hitting the glass—*bang*—they were birds hitting the glass and they were birds that had hit the glass and were dead. And *bang*, and *bang*, until nine caramels lay spilled and broken on the floor before the window. The impact of the window had unformed them. Their waxed-paper wrappers had burst in a few places, and brown oozed onto the polished tiles of the floor, the tiles that Zap himself had swept earlier.

Bang. Bang. Bang.

Someone was rattling the doors.

"Closed," Zap called without turning.

"Looks open to me."

It was the old guy.

"Are you deaf?" Zap said.

The old guy ignored him and started making his way toward Enzo's table as if it were his own. Joseph looked at the floor, which was littered with caramels.

"It's a goddamn obstacle course here," the old guy said.

Shuffle. Shuffle. Shuffle. The old guy could have used a walker, but he didn't. He made his way from table to table, gripping the corner of each for support, or the back of a chair. Eventually, he stood before them. He studied the new sign above Enzo's table. NO BANGING OF WRITING IMPLEMENTS ON TABLETOPS. THIS MEANS YOU, ENZO.

"Who the hell's Enzo?"

No answer. The old guy studied the sign again.

"He sounds like a pain in the ass, whoever he is," he said, and laughed. He had a laugh that Joseph wouldn't have expected, a high wheeze that made it sound as if he were gasping for air.

"She," Zap said.

"She? In what world is Enzo a woman's name?"

"In this one," Zap said. "It's her father's name. He wanted a boy."

"She, then," the old guy said. "Who is she?"

Zap shook his head. Too much to tell. Too much the old guy didn't know.

"She sounds like a pain in the ass," the old guy said again. He nodded at Joseph. "Just like this kid here."

"You know Flying Joseph?"

"I know the kid, sure. He keeps me company in the pool."

Zap gazed at the old guy. Joseph could tell he was wondering if the old guy had senile dementia, like the old lady whose son brought her in once in awhile. "Here you go, Mother," the son would say. "You wait here while I get the muffins."

The old guy scuffed with his foot at one of the dead caramels littering the floor. "Ask him what happened to his legs, Candy Killer."

"My name is not Candy Killer."

"Tell that to the caramels," the old guy said. "Answer me. What happened to his legs?"

The old guy nodded at Joseph's thigh, where a small circle of red from the puncture wound had briefly bloomed. Zap shook his head and made a dismissing motion with his hand: The puncture was nothing, no hurt at all.

"What happened to his legs," Zap said, "is that he fell off a mountain."

The old guy waved his hand back and forth, erasing Zap's words.

"That's a goddamn lie."

"How the hell would you know?"

"Look at him," the old guy said. "You can tell."

Zap gazed at Joseph from across the counter. Joseph could feel Zap's gaze, but he could not meet it. The bees buzzed inside their hive.

"We're closed, Old Man," Zap said. "Time for you to go home."

"Not before I get my lemon square."

A single shake of Zap's head, and the old guy shook his head and laughed.

"You're a hard-ass, aren't you?" he said. "I admire that in a kid."

Then he was making his way to the door, one small step at

a time. Hand over hand, from chair to chair. Zap gazed at Joseph. He, Zap, was in solidarity with Joseph, ready to fight the forces of evil.

"So," Zap said after a long time of willing Joseph to look at him and Joseph resisting that will. "What is up with you and that old man?"

"What is up with you and Enzo?"

Zap picked up a bruised and oozing Auntie Apple's caramel from the floor and dropped it back into the bowl. Picked it up. Dropped it.

"She's my sister," he said.

Zap crouched and his hands scrabbled over the tiled floor and scooped up the dead caramels. He tossed one up and down and did not look at Joseph.

"We have the same mother," he said. "The Figurehead and her split up when I was three. She had Enzo when I was eight, with my stepfather. I moved out three years ago."

Now Zap was juggling the broken Auntie Apple's caramels.

" 'If you leave this house, you are not our child.' That was their big threat."

Caramels tumbled through the air, and without looking, Zap caught one and tossed another, caught and tossed, caught and tossed.

"But they followed through on it. I'll give them that. They followed through."

Zap's hands were big and his fingers were slender and he tossed and caught, tossed and caught.

"I don't know what they told her when I left," Zap said.

"I don't know what she must have thought. I was the one who took care of her."

Broken caramels flew quietly through the air. Catchandtoss. Catchandtoss.

"I couldn't take her with me," Zap said. "And there is no way she could understand that."

In Joseph's mind, Enzo stood before him with her eyes glaring and her fists clenched, words with exclamation points behind them leaping from her mouth. Zap caught and tossed, caught and tossed.

"And now who takes care of her?" Zap said. "Do they even know it's summer and she's not in school? Look at her. With that ribbon and that watch. My God. It's so fucking pathetic."

Now he was juggling two Auntie Apple's caramels in each hand at once, as if two were one. Still his hands barely moved.

"As a brother, I'm a piece of shit."

Zap was crying.

"You're the one who should be her brother," he said. "I failed her."

"I failed, too," Joseph said.

"You fell," Zap said. "There's a big difference."

Before he fell, Joseph had made his way to the edge of the cliff. There was nowhere to go but into the ether, and down through the ether, to where the bright sea curled and uncurled over the boulder. He had not drifted through the clouds like Enzo imagined, and he had not been pillowed by the air, and he had not floated into warm water that held neon fish darting among the coral. He had not had time or distance to lean forward the way the ski jumpers did, their arms pressed to their sides, their eyes on the approaching cradle of snow. Joseph could not even remember the fall, so short had it been, and brutal.

"I miss my sister," Zap said. "I used to go by her Sunday-school class and look in the window to see if she would look up, so I could wave to her."

Joseph nodded.

"I miss my mother," he said.

Zap put his head down on folded arms. The crumpled ribbon sat in Zap's lap along with the paper-clip necklace that he had scooped from the sidewalk. The broken watch hung from his wrist. Zap opened his eyes and gazed at it, the one-handed watch with its crazed face, and he handed it over to Joseph.

Fourteen

In the three days that Joseph had not been to the pool, the old guy had crossed over to Joseph's side and made his way into enemy territory. Now he sat on the front line and gazed at Joseph. He cradled a palmful of water and stroked it down his skinny thigh, then cradled a palmful in the other hand and stroked it down the other thigh.

"Und so, vee meet again," the old guy said, in the voice of an old war-movie villain.

Joseph rolled himself over to the old guy's side of the pool. Now he himself was in enemy territory. An eye for an eye. He shoved himself from the chair directly into the water: Nothing, and then the cold was burning his middle.

"Kid."

"My name isn't Kid."

"And my name isn't Old Guy."

Joseph pushed himself off from the side with both arms and the lights burned down from above with their watery halos. Arms out. And in. But Joseph couldn't get his breath. He surfaced and hung by the side, laid his face sideways in the sloshing water of the pool filter. Then he hauled himself out and hoisted himself into his chair. Water dripped and made a puddle beneath him. Chlorine burned his sinuses.

The old guy stood up and his fists started to come together. He began to haul his body together into a semblance of the Unknown Stallone.

"I didn't used to be old like this."

"I didn't used to be in a chair."

The old guy's fists came down. His hands hung at the sides of his skinny thighs. Being on Joseph's side of the pool made him look older than he usually did. Or maybe something had changed here, too, and the old guy was getting older faster.

"So it's come to this," the old guy said. "Your chair versus my oldness."

He laughed. "Jesus," he said. "We're a coupla assholes."

The old guy raised his skinny arms above his head. Flying Joseph Meets the Unknown Stallone. His hands clenched into blue-veined fists. Joseph looked at his own arms, long and muscled and draped over the sides of his chair. Who would want to be Joseph's girlfriend? No one would want to be Joseph's girlfriend, Joseph who had no idea even how to kiss a girl. *I'm John Schaefer, nice to meet you. You can still have sex.* Like that was all that mattered. But Joseph didn't even know how to talk to a girl, even a girl he had gone to school with his entire life, a girl like Anna Micciolini.

Did you know anything about Joseph's mother?

Is she the one he was always with, the one in the dark coat?

Yes.

She's weird. They went to the playground a lot. She was always swinging. The little kids would freak out and he would try to get her away.

How did he do that?

I don't know. Stand by her and talk to her, I guess. Just hold her coat and talk to her.

And would she go with him?

After awhile. After awhile she would go with him.

Would Joseph's mother have the capability of hurting Joseph, in your opinion?

I don't know.

In your opinion, though?

Well anyone can hurt anyone, can't they?

Had she said that? There had been conversations between Anna and the investigators. Joseph didn't know what they had said to one another. He could only guess.

"You crying?"

The old guy's voice was close. He had made his way around the pool again, back into his own territory, which was now Joseph's territory, enemy territory. They had come full circle.

"Let me tell you something," he said. "I told my wife to shut up once. It was near the end. She wouldn't stop babbling. She had no idea who I was."

The old guy was standing next to Joseph's chair and he was so close that Joseph could see his blue veins, could see the sparse black hairs of his legs, his drooping belly.

"That's what I hope, anyway," the old guy said. "I can only hope she had no idea who I was when I told her to shut up."

The old guy's fingers reached for the broken watch.

"What's that you got there?"

The old guy was going to touch Enzo's watch. He would take it, and hold it, and gaze at it. His fingers would close over its brokenness. Joseph's hand convulsed and then he was staring at the blue water of the deep end of the pool, closing over the watch. The watch drifted to the bottom of the tiled floor, lurched forward once, and then lay still.

Joseph threw himself from his braked chair into the water.

Kid. The old guy's voice came to Joseph through the blue. *Kid.* It echoed, watery and burbling, into Joseph's ears as he forced himself with his arms to the bottom of the pool. The watch was there, and then it wasn't there. Blue wavered over the watch and Joseph could not get his fingers around it. He watched his fingers claw their way through the water to get to the watch; the fingers reached and stretched and tore for the watch.

Kid.

Joseph's arms propelled him to the surface of the pool and bellows forced air into his lungs and he was shoving off from the side again with his arms, diving down backward into the blue, and then spinning so that his head faced downward, and forcing his arms through the water toward the watch. His ears hurt from the pressure of the water. The water churned with the force of Joseph's arms, turned from blue to translucent bubbles rising around him, and water washed over the watch at the bottom of the pool, and the watch lay stilled and broken.

Jab.

Joseph saw through the blur a long stick coming at him.

Jab. The stick jabbed at him. His stomach, his chest, his head. His legs. Joseph turned in the water and forced himself down again, but the stick came after him and he saw it jab his legs.

Joseph rose.

His arms hung over the side of the pool, and his lungs burned. The old guy stood by the side of the pool, gripping one of the rescue poles in both hands. His hands were shaking and the pole was shaking.

"Jesus Christ, Kid. What the hell's wrong with you?"

The old guy was panting. His yellow bathing cap was nearly off his head, revealing his bald scalp.

"The watch," Joseph said. He turned back to the water and stared down through, trying to see the watch. Now he saw the watch. Now he didn't see it.

"Who gives a crap about the goddamn watch?"

"It's Enzo's watch."

Joseph peered through the blue and saw the watch. Now he didn't. Now he did.

"You fell off the side of this goddamn pool like you were dropping off a cliff," the old guy said. "And now you tell me it was a goddamn watch? Let me tell you something. There are plenty of other watches in this goddamn world. I thought you were drowning down there."

"You don't get it," Joseph said.

"I do get it. You think I could have gone in there and saved you?" The old guy pointed to his skinny chest. "The answer is no. I am not a superhero."

The old guy sank to a crouch, and then with difficulty sat next to Joseph on the edge of the pool.

"Now," the old guy said. "You tell me your name."

Joseph leaned his head sideways, so that the water sloshing in and out of the pool filter also sloshed in and out of his ear.

"My name is Joseph."

"And you tell me what happened to you."

Joseph's legs hung in the water, suspended by his arms on the side of the pool, and the smell of chlorine was pervasive.

"Your mother hurt you, didn't she?"

"No."

"You lie."

"She didn't mean to hurt me."

"But she did. Am I right?"

Back on the island, the bees had broken loose from the hive and were swarming by the bright water, and there was no one to calm them, no one to hold back their frustration and fear. The old guy sat on the rim of the pool with his yellow bathing cap askew. Joseph looked at him, and the image of a woman passed before him, obscured the old guy's face, an old woman who used to wear a yellow bathing cap.

"She thought she was saving me," Joseph said.

"From what?"

From what? From the forces of evil. From the people who waited in the wings for the weeks and months when she flushed her pills. From the people who were coming to get her and her son. From the people who ate bananas, but they weren't really bananas. From the people who put the milk in the cartons but it wasn't really milk. From the people on the street who looked like ordinary people but were not ordinary people, not at all. They were transmitting paralyzing rays from the fillings in their teeth, which were not really fillings. Joseph's mother was trying to get away from the men who wore dark suits, but the dark suits had one tiny thread of silver, somewhere in the jacket, somewhere near the pocket, somewhere you could hardly see it, somewhere no one but his mother could see it. But she could see it. She had the power. And the thread of silver meant that they were the ones. And the men in the suits with the threads of silver held rocks in their hands, and the rocks were aimed at Joseph's mother.

"I couldn't take care of her," Joseph said.

"Who?"

"My mother."

"Welcome to the world," the old guy said. "I couldn't take care of my wife, either."

"She's mentally ill," Joseph said.

The old man's hand still trembled from the effort with the pole.

"They used to call her a monster," Joseph said. "They were going to throw stones at her."

Joseph peered through the water at the watch at the bottom of the cement prison. Now it was there. Now it wasn't.

"And she got confused and she thought I was one of them."

The old guy nodded.

"And that is how she hurt you," he said. "All right. I release you."

The old guy lowered himself into the pool. He started doing his slow old-guy crawl, yellow cap barely clinging to his bald scalp, and then Joseph pushed off again from the wall and started his breaststroke, and they swam in opposite directions, toward each other and away from each other, toward and away, until the yawning man came in and flicked the lights up and down, because the gym was closing.

"Joseph?"

It was Mai, waiting for him.

"What are you doing here?"

"The bike kids found me at the playground earlier and said you almost died."

She stood against the brick wall. Next to her, the hydrangea bushes loomed, their giant flowers like popcorn balls in the darkness.

"But you're all right, aren't you? You don't seem hurt."

"I fell," Joseph said.

She stepped forward from the wall. He saw that she had been worried, and now she was seeing him in his familiar chair, damp and smelling of chlorine from the pool. He watched as the lines of her shoulders and her neck and her back eased, softened into her usual calm.

"Where'd you fall? Don't tell me off another mountain."

In the darkness, heavy and soft with humidity, Joseph couldn't see her eyes. Was she smiling? She was smiling. She lifted her spread fingers through her hair and let it fall back against her shoulder. Joseph's hands wanted to reach out and touch her, stroke the skin of her arm, haloed from the street-lamp; instead, he clasped the arms of his chair.

"Mai?"

He needed to say her name. She raised her eyebrows.

"Yes, Joey?"

"Did you just call me Joey?"

"Maybe."

"Are you teasing me?"

"Never. I would never do that. I'm not that kind of girl."

"Are you sure?" Joseph said. "Because it looks as if you are."

These were the kinds of things that Zap would say, not Joseph. But they were coming out of Joseph's mouth, and they were easy to say.

"Did you fall, though, this afternoon?" Mai said. "Really?"

"Yes."

"Why?"

"Fall," John Schaefer had said. "Just fall. Make yourself fall. It's not that big a deal." Sidewalk heaves and rough curb cuts and too-steep ramps and rocks in the road—the physical world was full of reasons to fall.

"I don't know why," Joseph said.

"Because Enzo is a crazy girl?" Mai offered. "Because she finally drove you over the edge?"

"Enzo's not crazy. She just wants things not to be the way they are."

"That's the good thing about being my brother. He doesn't think about things like that. He doesn't plan for the future."

"He doesn't have regrets, then."

"No," Mai said. "And no hope, either. Except to return to the ship."

She placed her hands in the air on an invisible rudder and tautened her body, staring straight ahead as if she were Cha, scanning the horizon. Cha, gazing out to sea. Joseph imagined Cha as he was not, a winged creature, flying in the dark night sky over the waves of an unseen ocean. Welcome, Captain.

"Maybe I'm wrong, though," she said. "How can I really know what goes through his mind?"

Then, in a single smooth motion, she was crouching next to Joseph. He could feel the electricity rising from her, gathering within. There was something she wanted to say to him, something she wanted to tell him. Her voice was quick and uncertain.

"Joseph—"

He leaned forward. She leaned forward, too, and her lips were on his. He smelled the citrus scent of her hair, and her cheek was soft and brushed against his cheek. Zap had been wrong. There was no need for Mai to tip her head upside down.

Fifteen

The days were growing shorter, in the waning weeks of summer, and dusk came earlier. Enzo had not appeared since the day Joseph fell out of his chair. Joseph pushed himself over the hump of the double doorsill, at closing, and the child rose from the shadows, from the hydrangea bushes, and stood before him.

"Where have you been?" Joseph said.

"Why do you care?"

"I was worried about you."

"No you weren't."

"I missed you."

"No you didn't."

Joseph reached his hand toward her—Please, talk to me—but she flinched away.

"What is that in your hair?"

She was a glittering child, her curls strung through with what looked like glimmering shards of shattered glass.

"Are those Zap's reading glasses? All crunched up?"

Enzo looked straight back at him, her hair gleaming coldly in the glare of the streetlight. Metallic fireflies. Her eyes were on his right hand.

"Where's my watch?"

"Gone."

"Gone where?"

"The bottom of the pool."

Her fingers curled around themselves.

"I don't care," she said. "I hated that watch anyway. It was the stupidest watch in the world."

Joseph said nothing. Her right hand scrubbed up and down her thigh, fingers open and searching, for what, Joseph didn't know. She was not carrying her clickster, and without it her hands didn't know what to do with themselves.

"Come inside with me," Joseph said.

"It's too late," she said. "The bakery closes at eight. Don't you remember? Are you retarded?"

Joseph fished in the pocket of his jeans and brought out the key—an ordinary silver key with a triangular head, dangling from a piece of bakery string. It revolved before her and she looked at it with distaste.

"It's too late," Enzo said again.

It was dusk, and the air was heavy with the scent of a nameless flower. Enzo's heart was skittering around inside her chest; Joseph could feel it as if it were his own. He felt himself back in the pool the night of the lost watch, heavy with chlorine and the repeated effort of throwing himself down into the water, trying to retrieve Enzo's watch. Now she was a child without time, a child of edgy, sparking energy. The rising cloud of her dark hair glittered, strung through with brokenness. The air around them was growing darker.

A movement behind the closed windows of the bakery caught Joseph's eye and he knew without gazing directly that it was Zap, moving among the tables, sweeping the already-swept floor, arranging the salt and pepper shakers and sugar bowls in an exact trinity in the middle of each table, moving in a restless pattern of his own making.

Now Zap was standing beside the post at the far window, the window that Kilt Man gazed through each day. He was only feet from Enzo and Joseph. Zap was listening; Joseph could feel him listening.

"You're hurt," Enzo said. "You're hurt everywhere."

Enzo pointed at his thigh, where his jeans covered the bandage she couldn't see.

"You're going to keep on getting hurt," Enzo said. "It's never going to stop."

"Where's your clickster?"

She pulled it out of her pocket, as if she had been waiting for him to ask, and he watched her fingers close around it in relief. Then she drew a line through the air with her finger, outlining the circumference of his body and the wheelchair, too. Now Joseph was in a bubble, an invisible bubble shield. Now Joseph was protected by Enzo. She held the clickster steady, as if the power of the invisible shield flowed directly from her, through the clickster, and around Joseph. Behind the window, Zap moved, a small movement. He was leaning against the glass now, staring out at them.

"You lied to me," Enzo said. "You told me that the island was an island of bees."

"No. I didn't."

"You said that the sun always shone and there were palm trees and coconuts and the sand was white and the ocean was warm and that your little sister was always happy."

"You said that. Not me. I'm from upstate New York. The islands there are rocky and the sand is brown and everything is covered with snow all winter long."

"But that's not the kind of island I want! I want your island. With palm trees and coconuts and a jungle and bananas, and rocks to keep out the pirates."

"That island doesn't exist," Joseph said.

The clickster trembled in the air. She wanted to be powerful, to be armed against those who would do her and those she loved harm, but the force was weakening.

"Enzo. Do you want to know the whole truth?"

Her hand stilled.

"I didn't fall off a mountain. My mother pushed me off a slide."

She waited. Fragments of broken reading glasses, stem and frame and lenses, jeweled and sequinned, made her look like a child in a costume. A child worker in a circus for the insane.

"The kids at the playground were throwing rocks at her," Joseph said. "She climbed up the slide at the pool to get away from them. And I climbed up after her to try to get her down."

"Why were they throwing rocks at her?"

"They thought she was a monster."

"Is she?"

"She's mentally ill," Joseph said. "She needs to swing on a swing every day. She stands guard over the wading pool. She believes that there are people in the world out to get her, plotting against her. She thinks she can hear birds talking."

"Big said she was in a hospital. She can't swing every day if she's in a hospital, can she?"

"No. No, she can't."

"So you just left her back there by herself, when she's sick and she can't take care of herself?"

"I didn't want to leave her."

"But you did."

"Yes," Joseph said. "I did."

Joseph had not wanted to leave his mother, but they had taken his mother away from him. Enzo longed for the island of her mind, the island where children did not leave their parents and where brothers stayed with their sisters. Enzo would hear only the words *left her back there by herself,* and she would clutch them close, write them on the air with her clickster, worry them into her bones.

"Do you write to her?"

"I write to her."

"And does she get your letters? Does she write back?"

Joseph saw what she wanted, which were letters back and forth, letters crossing in midair east to west, letters filled with news of the flatlands and news of the island, letters filled with chatty love. A five-dollar bill on a birthday. Hugs and kisses.

"No," Joseph said. "She doesn't."

"Why not?"

"She takes a lot of medicine now," Joseph said.

"So she'll get better, then."

In Enzo world, medicine would make his mother better. When the illness had first begun, Joseph was young and he knew that his mother would get better. They would find the right medicine, and his mother would take it, and one morning he would wake up and she would be in the kitchen making bacon and pancakes with corn in them, her specialty. And in the meantime Joseph could keep his mother calm. He could keep her to her routine, her routine of playground and Scrabble and lemon squares and butter-spread saltines.

"Right? She'll get better."

"I don't know," Joseph said. "People don't always get better."

Joseph's mother was a woman in a dark coat who stood in a kitchen, gazing out the window. Her fingers were raw and scabbed. Old chlorine in Joseph's eyes burned and stung, old chlorine that had merged with the cells of his body. Joseph was part pool now, part of the water that waved itself over the watch at the bottom of the blue.

A bee bumbled its way out of the hydrangea bushes that grew next to the brick of the bakery. It was a plodding sort of bee, zigging this way and that. No purpose, no rhyme nor reason to its flight. It was a bee that had missed its chance during the height of summer and now found itself lacking.

Enzo still could not help herself: Every time she saw a bee she shrank away, and she shrank away now. The bee gathered itself, as if it had heard her, and flew in a straight path toward Joseph.

Joseph watched the bee land on his ankle, on the exposed flesh between his sock and the hem of his jeans. He watched as the bee lowered its tail, huddling itself purposefully into the white inner flesh, as if it had been waiting for this moment. Enzo's clickster described a frantic circle in the air.

"Make it stop. Kill it."

The clickster chattered. It was trying to warn Joseph of impending danger. Lead extended itself millimeter by millimeter. From where she stood on the pavement, Enzo was only a few feet away from the bee, from Joseph's leg, but she could not move.

"Joseph! I can see it stinging you!"

Joseph watched as the dark blot of the bee hunched, still and focused, over the flesh of his ankle.

"Are you alive in there? Wake up! Do something!"

Enzo waved the clickster frantically in the air between them. The bee, sated, dragged away from Joseph's ankle and hauled itself through the deepening sky.

Enzo leaped forward and stood before Joseph in his chair. Behind her, on the other side of the window, stood the shadowy and intent shape of Zap.

"It hurts," Enzo said, weeping. "It hurts. Look."

The clickster pointed to the sting. Already it was swelling, puffing in an angry red well around the micropoint of the sting. She reached toward him. The clickster dropped to the sidewalk, and she laid the back of her hand on Joseph's ankle. She shook her head and he saw but could not feel how she pressed her skin against the sting. Then it came to him what she was trying to do, which was absorb Joseph's pain into her own flesh, and he put his hand on her head. He smoothed her hair, fingers catching on the bits of broken glasses.

"You don't know," she said. "You don't know anything. They threw out all his stuff. When he left. They put it all in big black garbage bags and they put it out in the alley and the garbagemen came and took it away."

Enzo trembled and glittered before him. Where could it possibly fit, all the sadness and anger that Enzo held? It was not containable, and yet she stood before him, shimmering, not exploding, not flying into pieces.

"They threw away his music," Enzo said. "And his books. His notebooks, too—they threw them away. They threw away his clothes. Even the shirt with the tiger on it—they threw that away."

Her hands scrabbled up and down her legs. Someone had set fire to the hive and the bees were trapped inside and desperate for a way out.

"I used to sleep in that shirt!" Enzo said. "That was the shirt he gave me to sleep in!"

Her fingers fluttered in the air and wove themselves together, then apart. The bees were burning, their slender bodies singed. Her fingers were in her hair now, feeling through the tangles for the broken reading glasses, the beads and sequins and broken lenses falling to the ground.

"My brother moved out," she said. "And they threw everything away. And they didn't tell me he was going. And he didn't tell me he was going!"

The angry child squeezed her eyes together in fury and frustration.

"I want a brother!"

"You have one," Joseph said.

Enzo raised her clickster and wordlessly pointed at Joseph. Then she was off, down the dark sidewalk, her legs flashing white, the streetlamps one at a time haloing her head, her nimbus of dark curls. She reached the end of the block and sped right and disappeared. Nine years old was too young to be out this late. Joseph knew he should go after her, make sure she got home safely, wherever home was. But his hands on the tires shoved him in the other direction, and he began to glide west toward the lake.

Sixteen

A couple sat on the far playground bench, the one closest to the water, the bench that Mai liked to sit on when she came to the lake with the Captain, the swinging bench half-hidden by rosebushes. They looked to be about Joseph's age. The girl leaned into the boy, who wrapped his arms around her and rested his chin on the top of her head. Their whispered laughter drifted over the sand to the walking path, where Joseph shoved himself quickly past.

The moon had risen and cast a wide, glittering path across the water. It was a summer evening so still that the path of light looked almost solid, as if Joseph could shove himself across the sand and then roll across the water to the other side. Water, dense and pliable under the tires of his chair.

Joseph passed the pirate's ship and kept going. The air was so humid that it, too, seemed almost solid. Water and air felt animate tonight, as if they wanted to speak, as if there was something they needed to convey.

A tall man stood by the oak at the far end of the grass that bordered the beach by the playground. In the moonlight, Joseph could see his kilt. He gazed out at the water and Joseph followed his gaze.

Stones in the water.

The surface of the lake had drawn itself back, revealing the stones at its bottom, stones that stayed silent and still under the swimmers of the day, stones that in the hush of darkness unveiled themselves from their shroud of water. So many of them, and all the same size. The stones looked as if they were floating. Joseph had never seen such a sight. Maybe the water was, in fact, solid. Maybe the properties of the physical universe had been altered on this one night, and thrown stones floated.

Now Kilt Man touched the oak with one hand, and then pulled his hand away. He turned, as if Joseph had called his name. Across the expanse of sand that separated them, he gazed, and Joseph could sense the immensity of the sadness emanating from him, and he could not stand it, and he set his ungloved hands to his tires.

Joseph wheeled himself past the Tin Fish, shuttered and dark for the night, and up the incline to the overpass above the narrow channel that led to Lake of the Isles. The moon followed him, its path wider the longer he rolled. Joseph kept his eyes on the stones. They were still and rounded. And then the world swiveled itself a fraction of a millimeter and settled back in place, and Joseph saw that he was looking not at stones but at geese.

Geese turned their heads to the moon.

Joseph was an intruder, an alien in this world, interrupting communion at the church of the moon, the church of the lake.

He pushed himself up the path to the top of the overpass and stopped and looked back to the oak at the far edge of the sand. Was that Kilt Man's hand, touching lightly down upon the bark of the oak and lifting off again? Was he now tilting his head toward the moon, and now tilting back toward Joseph? Maybe he believed himself able to hear the thoughts of the geese. Maybe someone somewhere in this hushed city— a daughter, or a mother, someone who loved Kilt Man—was out searching.

The dark Minneapolis air pressed in on Joseph in its heavy way. He placed his fingers against his bee sting; the skin was hot and felt tight and shiny. He remembered what a bee sting felt like, the skewering pain, receding and then gathering itself again.

Enzo had pressed her flesh against Joseph's flesh, wanting to take away the pain. But there was no pain. Was there? If you couldn't feel it, did that mean it wasn't there? Mai's eyes were sad sometimes, and she did not tell him why. Enzo danced and shivered her angry way through the bakery. Cha's eyes were always calm.

For months, Joseph had imagined Anna Micciolini, the girl he had watched for years and spoken to only once. Was it possible to love a girl you had never touched, a girl you had spoken with only once, when you were lying in a hospital bed? He conjured her, the way he had conjured her for years.

Hi, Joseph.

"Hi, Anna."

She was wearing a T-shirt tonight. No parka with a ski tag hanging from the zipper. No pale sweater buttoned over another shirt.

"You look happy," he said. "You look pretty."

She smiled. *Thanks.*

"Anna?"

He wanted to tell her something. He wanted to tell her so much.

So, she said. *Mai.*

Anna stood before Joseph in the darkness, the thousand and more miles between upstate New York and Minneapolis reappearing and vanishing as she stood before him.

Good.

"Anna?"

Yes.

"My mother—"

She saw the look on his face and she bent over him and placed her hand on the flesh of his chest. He could feel her hand on his skin, cool and dry in this heavy, humid air. It had been six months and three weeks and six days since that day at the playground in upstate New York. The sun had glittered on the snow by the swing. Joseph could not bear it, could not bear that his best had not been enough, and there were other things he could not bear, either. A wave of grief came swarming up from Joseph's unfeeling toes and massed into his heart.

"Mountains," Joseph said. It was all he could say, and it made no sense. But she was listening carefully. She was listening the way Joseph used to listen to his mother's word salad. Anna was making sense of Joseph.

Mountains you won't hike, and stairs you won't climb and miles you won't run, and me who you won't ever see again.

"Yes," he said, and he thought *yes,* again, and the swarm rose within him and he gave up and let it rise. The bees were released inside him, and the bees rose from within his skin and pushed and pressed the heavy fur of their bodies against the inside of his pale skin, the skin he could feel and the skin he couldn't. The bees wanted out, and they would not be denied, and they rose right out of the cells of his skin, the oceans and mountains of his body. They were loosed upon the dark night air of the small room where Joseph sat trapped, and they gathered themselves and flew toward the screen, and they pushed themselves through the tiny holes they could not fit through, but they did fit through, and then they were gone, vanishing toward the moon.

You'll do other things, Anna said, and she gazed down at Joseph, and she took her hand away, and she was gone.

The doorbell rang, and rang again, and then the knocking began.

"Hey! You in there?"

Enzo. Joseph could hear her from the kitchen. She was standing outside the front bedroom window, which she thought was Joseph's.

"This is an expedition," she yelled. "We are once and for all going to find the creepy bird at Lake of the Isles. Get your butt out of bed."

It was the dying of summer and the beginning of fall, and falling gold leaves spun through the morning air. Joseph heard Big's window shove upward and he wheeled himself out of the kitchen and down the hall to the front door.

"Who the hell are you?"

"Who the hell are *you*?"

"You're a little kid. You shouldn't swear like that."

"You're a big beer guy. You shouldn't, either."

"You woke me up."

Joseph opened the door. Big was behind him now. Enzo gazed up at Big from the top of the ramp and nodded.

"It's late," she said. "Rise and shine. Up and at 'em!"

"I work nights."

"Lots of people do."

Enzo would not melt in front of Big. She would not tell him everything, or anything. She was the guardian of her world.

"So, Mr. Beer Guy, are you sorry about anything?" she said.

"How old are you?" he said in return.

Enzo shook her head. She had no use for adults who asked standard kid questions, questions regarding your grade in school, how your summer was going, what you had in your hand; all were met with a quick and definitive shake of Enzo's head.

"Are you sorry about Joseph's mother?" Enzo said.

"Don't talk about his mother."

"Too late for that."

Big passed a hand over his head and squeezed his temples.

"Why would I be?"

"Because you left her back there."

"I had to. It's a hospital."

"It's a prison hospital," Enzo said.

And it was. For someone who needed to swing every day, who every day needed to gaze into the children's wading pool, who needed to feel her son's fingers on the lapel of her dark coat, the place Joseph sent his letters to was a prison above and beyond its guards and its locked gates.

Enzo regarded him, this grown man, this oven guy, this man who had left his wife back in Utica. She poked Big in the shoulder with a stiff finger.

"Does that hurt?"

"You don't get it," Big said. "She used to be pretty."

Poke.

"Does it hurt now?"

"She used to be happy."

Poke.

"Now?"

"She used to be different," the beekeeper's father said. Joseph watched Enzo look up at his father. Way up. Enzo angled her finger up at the big man's face.

"Also, you left him," she said, and she swiveled her finger to point at Joseph. "Did you ever think of that?"

Enzo stared Big down, and after a time Big's head bowed down. The investigator had triumphed. Big had emerged from his dark world of window blinds and nighttime ovens into an interrogation room. If Joseph were a witness for the defense, what would he say? Would he tell them about the daily loaf of bread in its brown paper bag on the kitchen table? The bread, and the long bread knife, and the butter on its yellow plate. But the silent table with the bread and the knife and the Hope Creamery butter on the yellow dish would not matter to Enzo, Joseph knew, and so the witness for the defense remained silent. Big backed into the apartment and closed the door.

Seventeen

Cha stood at the prow of the ship. Mai sat across the playground, on the bench next to the tire swing, the bench that rocked. One foot braced itself against the child-safe rubbery surface of the playground and pushed off, and the other was tucked underneath her. Southwest High School's orientation was that evening. Zap had assured Joseph that Southwest had handicap ramps and elevators and that he, Zap, would be watching Joseph's back.

Zap and Enzo stood flanking Joseph's wheelchair. Zap had helped shove the chair through the sand of the 32nd Street beach to the water's edge of Lake Calhoun. On the opposite shore, three small maples had turned to orange. These three maples were like the swamp maples at home, back in the Utica floodplain.

Enzo gathered flat stones to skip. She came back with her fingers clutched around a fistful.

"If you could be a superhero—" Enzo said to Joseph, and looked at him. "*If*—what would your superpower be?"

"If I could be a superhero, *if*," Joseph said, "I would fly."

"*Fly?* Are you serious?"

"Yup."

"With tights and a cape?"

"No tights. No cape. Just the flying."

"But that's so boring!" Enzo said. "You can't want that to be your superpower!"

"I do, though," Joseph said.

If Enzo had had her clickster, she would have pointed it straight at Joseph's heart and clicked.

"I never thought you would turn out to be boring like this," Enzo said.

"What's boring about flying?" Joseph said. "How could anyone not want to fly? I've wanted to fly my whole life long."

Enzo shook her head. No paralyzing rays, no superstretching, no invisibility. Out of everything in the world, all he wanted was to fly? She jiggled the stones in her tucked-up shirt, then plucked one out and tossed it into the water. Plop. She tossed another one, and another.

" 'Boring Joseph,' " she said. "That's it, then?"

"That's it."

Enzo flung her last stone and went down the beach to gather more.

"So," Joseph said to Zap. "Did you really think that I fell off the side of a mountain?"

"No. Big had already told me what happened."

"Why didn't you say anything, then?"

Zap shrugged. "I figured it was your story to tell, if and when you felt like it."

Zap arced a stone out across the flat lake. Everything Zap did with his body was done with strength and grace. Joseph imagined him walking out onto the surface of the water; it would hold.

"Besides," Zap said, "who cares how you broke your neck? It's broken is all."

Another stone danced across the water, twirling and alighting, until Joseph blinked and it was gone.

"No one cares how the superhero got hurt," Zap said. "They only care about his superpower."

Another stone.

In a few months, Lake Calhoun would be frozen over. Zap had told Joseph that sometimes the city cleared a path around the perimeter of the entire lake, and that if that happened, Joseph would be able to chair around while he, Zap, skied next to him on the snow.

Enzo was back, the bottom of her shirt a makeshift basket sagging under the weight of the stones she had piled into it. She looked across the beach at Mai, who had lain down on the bench and closed her eyes.

"Is she your girlfriend?" Enzo said to Joseph.

"She could be," Zap said. "If Flying Joseph would get his head out of his butt long enough to notice that she likes him."

"Was I talking to you?" Enzo said. "No. I was talking to Boring Joseph. Boring Joseph, is Mai your girlfriend?"

"Yes," Joseph said. "Why yes, she is."

Joseph looked up at Zap, and Zap's eyes were surprised and Zap laughed and held out his hand for a high five.

"Well, I knew it," Enzo said. "I knew it."

She was back in the dark room with the spotlight shining down on her victim. She had been working on this case a long time, and her efforts had finally paid off.

"It's his shoulders," Zap said. "Women like big shoulders. And biceps. They like biceps, too."

"Who asked you?" Enzo said. "Who made you the expert on women?"

"It's common knowledge."

Zap's braids had bleached to the color of whipped honey over the summer. They were tied back with a pink Hello Kitty shoelace that Enzo had given him. Joseph had watched Enzo do the gathering and tying. Hello Kitty had no mouth. Hello Kitty's eyes gazed blankly ahead. Joseph sat in his chair, his fingertips grazing the rubber of the tires. He looked across the beach and across the playground at Mai, whose face was turned up to the sun. She pushed off with her big toe, pushed off and rocked gently. Across the sand of the playground, Cha gazed out to sea.

Enzo flung a stone into the lake. She tried to angle her arm in a wide arc so that the stone would skip, but she was terrible at skipping stones and the stone sank immediately.

"Enzo," Zap said. "Watch."

He reached over and plucked one of the long, flat stones from Enzo's pile. And his hand curved in toward his wrist, and his arm angled out to his side, and he arced the stone out over the glass-smooth lake. One. Two. Three. Four. Five.

"If I get good, I can use a rock to kill the creepy bird at Lake of the Isles," Enzo said. "Once we find it."

"You won't find the creepy bird," Zap said. "Loons don't like humans. And why should they, when small children want to kill them?"

Enzo flung another stone into the lake. It sank immediately.

"Is your mother's prison on an island?" Enzo said to Joseph. She plucked his handicap-button stick from its resting place between his leg and the chair, ready to scratch the answer in the sand or write it in the air. She was trying to give up her clickster, but she could not entirely give it up. Clickster substitutes were everywhere and the habit was deep within her.

"No."

"Where is it, then? Does she live on another planet?"

"Maybe."

"Where is her planet?"

Where was his mother's planet? His mother's planet was inside her. She lived in a galaxy of her own self, made of her bones and muscle and blood and whatever brains are made of. Whatever a heart is made of. Whatever a soul is made of.

"You don't know where your mother's planet is, then?" Enzo said. The handicap-button stick was poised and waiting in the sand.

"That's right."

"Are you telling me the truth?"

"Yes. I am telling you the truth."

"And she thought she was saving you from the forces of evil," Enzo said. This was a story they had gone through many times since the day Joseph fell from his wheelchair onto the sidewalk in front of the bakery.

"Yes."

"And did she?"

"Did she what?"

"Did she save you from the forces of evil?"

Zap arced another stone across the water. Joseph could see his mother, the way she had looked on top of the slide, after she had flung herself from the swing and clambered up the bars. She had crouched. She had swiveled her head, keeping track of the children who surrounded her at a distance of yards, afraid to approach her. She had murmured Joseph's name over and over, telling him that she would keep him safe from these forces of evil. She would protect him. Joseph's voice had murmured back, an eddying stream of slow words. Given enough time, he could have coaxed her safely down. Given enough time, his mother would have heard him. Given enough time, his mother would have turned her head toward him and locked her eyes with his.

"I didn't have enough time," Joseph said.

His mother had not heard Joseph climbing up the slide behind her. He had reached out and touched her dark coat, brushed it with his fingertips the way he always did when she was lost. He had kept murmuring, washing her with warm words, waves of whispered words breaking and receding over the electric hunch of her body.

"You're not answering my question," Enzo said.

When Joseph's mother had turned, she had been fast. She had whipped about, and her fist was already clenched and ready. His mother's unexpected strength, Joseph's own shock, and the force of gravity had combined. He had arced backward. His fingers had clutched for a handhold, but there was no handhold.

"Was she or was she not saving you from the forces of evil?"

"In her mind, she was," Joseph said.

The bars of the stairs of the slide had caught him at the back of his head, and he had toppled down and then toppled again into the emptied pool. When Joseph had opened his eyes, his mother was gazing down from the slide, her fist still clenched. Her eyes had not widened so much as narrowed, shrunk, gathered all the available light in her vision into two piercing rays. When she saw what she had done, she had stood straight up on the slide and leaped. The sand beneath was soft under the bright snow, and it had caught her, and held her, and she had stayed motionless until they came to get her, and took her to the place where she was now, and where she would be for a long time.

"Well," Enzo said. "At least she wasn't a supervillain."

Joseph looked at Enzo, who was standing in the sand. Her hair, too, had grown longer over the summer, dark curls hanging to her shoulders, strands glinting red and blue and blond in the sun.

"Don't you want to know what my superpower would be?" she said.

Now she leaned on her stick, the words she scratched out in the sand unintelligible.

"Let me guess," Zap said. "You'd be a bee wrangler. Round them up and pen them in."

"Nope."

She looked at Joseph.

"Aren't *you* going to guess?"

"Not flying," Joseph said. "Since according to you, flying would be so boring. That's my guess."

"Not flying? That's not a real guess. That's a not guess."

"You tell me, then."

Enzo leaned on Joseph's handicap-button stick, which was bending under her slight weight. Soon it would snap. Joseph imagined her losing her balance, falling to the sand, the jagged edges of broken stick pushing through her tanned skin. He closed his eyes and opened them again; still she stood, the branch long and unbroken.

She stood up straight and yanked it from the sand.

"You can't guess?" she said.

He shook his head. She pointed the stick at his legs, his legs in their jeans in the chair.

"I'll tell you, then," she said. "My superpower would be you, back in time, before that stupid slide. You, Joseph, unfalling."

Back in time, before that stupid slide. Had Joseph spoken to Anna Micciolini years ago, she might have spoken back to him. She might have smiled at him. She might have held his hand. If Joseph had been able to speak, if Joseph had been able to save his mother, if Joseph had fallen not onto his head but onto his knees, if he had fallen onto his knees. If he had never fallen at all, if he were back in time, back. In time.

"That would mean undoing my life," Joseph said.

"Just that part of it."

"Then your life is undone, too, little sister," Zap said. "No Joseph here in Minneapolis. Ever think of that?"

Enzo looked at Zap and nodded, once, a tiny motion that bespoke her thoughts: Yes, she had thought about that. Yes, she knew the consequences. The investigator had done her homework, figured out the ramifications, knew that in order for the beekeeper to gain, the Mighty Thor must lose.

"But his legs wouldn't be hurt," Enzo said. "Ever think of that?"

Joseph looked across the sand, across the playground, to the top of the pirate ship, where Cha stood before the red rudder and gazed out to sea, the inland sea of Lake Calhoun, where his journey was taking place. In time, slow thunder and shivers of lightning would bruise the horizon. Storms would blow in and pockmark the steely surface of the water. Food would be scarce. Huge fish might come boiling up from the depths in the middle of the sea and threaten to overturn Cha's small ship. Strange birds would cry from somewhere in the darkness, and he would not know where they were or if they meant him harm. Stones would lie silent on the ocean floor. Boulders would jut from the blue, blue sea, and the danger of foundering upon them would be real, but the child would stay the course.

If his legs were not hurt, Joseph would rise and walk across the sand. He would reach out and take the ropes of the rope ladder in his hands. He would haul himself up to the tiny captain's lookout and crouch next to Cha, Cha, whose hands hovered now above the spokes. Joseph sat in his chair, his life lifting before him.

"No," Joseph said. "This is where I am now."

Acknowledgments

Thanks and love to M. T. Anderson, Kate DiCamillo, Julie Schumacher, Darin Smith, and Brad Zellar, all of whom were of great help with this novel. The same to Doug Stewart, agent and kindred spirit, and the brilliant Frances Coady, she of the great laugh and unerring instinct. More thanks to Eric Luoma, whose Bellwether voice was a musical muse for many months, and to Peter Kelsey, owner of the New French Bakery. I am grateful to several health professionals who helped me with practical information and medical details, including nurse practitioner Jackie Higgins, librarian Mary Carlson, pathologist Gary Carlson, and neurologist Richard Zarling. Deepest gratitude to Tim Vraa and Paula Duggan Vraa, who shared so generously of their experience.